A GLIMPSE OF PARADISE

I

A GLIMPSE OF PARADISE

by

Louise Bourdon

II

A GLIMPSE OF PARADISE

Copyright © Louise Bourdon 2025

DEDICATION

This book is dedicated to all the brave angels who left too soon; they will never be forgotten, for they live on in these pages I have written.

This is in honour of their memory.

HEAR MY WORDS

The words that you read throughout this book are only those that come from my mind. It may not be of great comfort to all that read, but it is a great comfort to me.

We can only hope that heaven is as beautiful as what I describe in this book, for we do not know what exactly we will find when we reach the other side.

My vision is my vision, and when your time comes, you are more than welcome to join me there.

One day, we will be at peace. We will be free. We will be at rest.

Louise

X

AUTHOR'S PREFACE

Several of my loved ones have gone to be with God, and in this book, I have written about many of them, although I have changed their names. My nans and grandads, my aunties and uncles, friends, my stepdads, and my dad.

With my strong faith and beliefs in the afterlife, I have taken what I hope to find when I go to heaven, and made it into a story.

I understand it will not be for everyone, and you may even ask yourself questions such as, 'Is this really how it is believed to be?'

Well, I believe in heaven and although I do not know what I will find when I get there, this is how I am picturing it to be like and remember, this is a story. I understand I can never make others believe what I believe, I can only write about what I envisage it to be myself and I hope that by reading my book, it will give you great comfort and uplift you in the same way as it has me.

So, if you are wondering, 'Is Heaven real?'

Remember, it is as real as you want it to be….

I hope you find peace and comfort in reading this book.   Louise x

SEE YOU LATER

You are unable to be seen,

for you are deep-rooted in a faraway place that I
cannot reach.

I tried so hard to hold you back, but it was your time.

You are not lost, though, for I feel your presence, and
I hear you in my mind.

I know, you are on the other side,

smiling at me, telling me that you have just gone on
ahead.

So, I smile back and say,

'See you later.'

-Louise Bourdon

PROLOGUE

It had been three months since Will Devoir had died after a very short illness. He was never one for ever talking about heaven or whether he even believed in it, but shortly after he passed, he began to reach out to Eloise from the 'other side.' Sending her signs, whether it be a butterfly, a robin or the brightest shining star. These all gave her hope and comfort in her grieving and made her feel close to him. She was thankful for her faith, knowing that one day she would be with her love again, and that was all she had left to hold on to.

But as days turned into weeks and weeks into months, every day without Will became harder and harder. She struggled to move on in life until finally, she could no longer be without the man she loved….

CHAPTER 1

It was a bitterly cold December night. A curtain of glistening snow rolled over the hills as a brisk wind blew out of the midnight sky and swept across the land. Appledore was known for having the worst winters, mainly because it stood in the North where the Taw and Torridge rivers met before they drifted into the Atlantic, at Bideford Bay. But perched on a hillside, this quaint fishing village was as enchanting as its name. Characterised by its winding narrow streets and an attractive jumble of closely packed cottages painted in different pastel hues, each cottage stood proud, facing each other across cobbled courtyards. Their frontages hung with baskets of overflowing flowers, making Appledore the most perfect place to live, with a neighbourly atmosphere where residents looked out for one another. Despite the winter weather, it was a picturesque village, with a peaceful atmosphere and tranquil surroundings, not forgetting the home of arguably the best ice cream in Devon.

A harsh wind whistled through the open vent in Eloise Darlington's bedroom, like a ghost chillingly breathing through cracks in a wall. No matter how many attempts she had made to try to close it, it was stuck for good, and not being much of a 'diy' expert, she had not the faintest idea on how to fix it, although pasting layers of newspaper in the gaps of the vent was only a temporary measure, it did not however stop the cold air blowing through. Moonstone Cottage was a cosy, petite cottage in a quaint little street, and a stone's throw from the beach. It appeared to need attention in several places, including the overgrown jungle of a garden, but now was not really the time to be worrying about such small things. In fact, the cottage itself, being very quaint, was very old and a lot of things either did not work or creaked, but the open tread wooden stairs and the quirky sloped ceilings made up for all the items that needed repairing, and she was grateful for the comforting touches throughout that made it her home. The log fire would normally be burning away in her bedroom by now, except it had clearly slipped her mind to collect fresh logs from the woodshed earlier on, one of her many chores that she seemed lately to forget to do, and being a small cottage, she very rarely had to worry about keeping it warm.

After a restless night of tossing and turning along with the bleak thoughts that kept swirling around in her head, Eloise Darlington was still wide awake. Her pills still sat on her bedside cabinet from the night before. She contemplated whether to take them or not, whilst her headache still pounded from the previous day, from lack of sleep over the past few months. She was never one for getting a good night's sleep; in fact, she was not quite sure of the last time she had slept through a whole night, as it was not something she had managed for a while. Bitterly cold, she wrapped herself in her duvet like a lost soul, overwhelmed by the thoughts inside her head, the same thoughts that had kept her awake every single night for the past three months. Her mind turned to her love, as tears began rolling down her cheeks once again.

Will Devoir was the love of her life. They had first chatted online after both had taken part in the same video conference. It turned out they worked for the same company, but in different offices in different areas! Neither of them had spoken to each other before, and it was only when Will had written a post about the conference and Eloise had responded to it that they soon got chatting online. Soon, they were video calling one another regularly, and the moment she first spoke to him, she felt as if her whole world had lit up, because never in a million years did she ever imagine falling in love so quickly. They met up a few times, with Will staying at Eloise's often. He lived in Bristol at the time, a good two hours away, and very busy compared to the quaint and peaceful village that she lived in. They connected immediately, as if they were able to read one another's thoughts! Thinking and feeling the same, and their stares into each other's eyes continued from the very first day they spoke online, to the first time they met up, and there was no turning back. Will was 24, eight years younger than Eloise, when they first got together, and she had often joked about him being her toy boy. Funny, very quick-witted with a smile that lit up the room, and an infectious laugh that lifted her every time, but it was his gigantic heart that filled her with happiness, being the kindest and most loving man she had ever known. Although they had been through a lot in their lives, they always managed to get through the other side, making them stronger by the day, which only brought them closer, making their love for one another deeper. Twenty years later, and they had still been going strong.

The day Will was rushed into the hospital was a day she would never forget. It was a weekend, and he had decided to catch up on some work at home. Being a Computer and Information Systems Manager put a lot of pressure on Will, as he had been responsible for the whole of the company's computer systems. It was down to him to analyse every computer in the company and recommend upgrades, and if anything went wrong, it was on his shoulders. Having considered many times about a change in career, something Eloise had suggested, maybe a job a little less stressful, it never happened, as this was something he had done since he had left uni. All those years of hard work and exams to get the qualification he needed; it was all he knew, even if some days he had not been getting home until 8 pm, it was not something he wanted to give up on now.

The day was full of snow, and the icy wind blew a gale as she had set off that morning. Leaving Will to catch up with his father, Maurice, meant she did not have to rush back. The skies above were an unholy mixture of pale grey clouds as they hovered in the winter's sky, whilst the snow crunched under her boots as she walked, and as the snow pelted her face, and the cold air stung her cheeks, she wrapped her scarf up around her to further shield her from the bitter weather. Having chosen to walk meant she did not have to worry about scraping the ice off the car beforehand, waiting for it to heat up, or looking for a space to park, for there were always limited spaces, especially at weekends, although the day was one of those days she wished she had stayed in the warm, snuggled under her duvet with her fingers wrapped around a cup of hot cocoa.

The village was a serene haven of delight and tranquillity, offering a peaceful life, and around every corner stood a vision of kind and welcoming people. At the zebra crossing, a very sweet lady stopped in her car, and smiled as she crossed, being careful not to slip on the icy road, she put up her hand to say thank you and went on her way. For a small village, Appledore had a vast choice of facilities, even though it was rare for a village to be so blessed with such an excellent array of independent shops and eateries. Marchlands was a well-respected local establishment, with a grocery shop, a mouth-watering selection of deli food, and a very welcoming café, and Eloise spent most of her time at this mall as she felt it always had everything that she needed all in one place, rather than looking around at several different shops, and it taking twice as long. Herself and Will had regularly stopped by at the Felton's café for their usual hot chocolate and croissant, which Eloise had always highly recommended to the locals in the village. They sold the finest coffee too, from all over the world, and the atmosphere within always made the café very inviting. Kate Felton was the owner, short, with neatly trimmed chestnut brown hair, and quite stylish too. A sweet little lady who had been running the cafe for many years, previously owned by her parents, she had taken over after they had decided to take early retirement. Eloise's arm raised in the direction of the café as she waved at her dear friend, and as Kate returned the wave with a smile, Eloise continued in the mall as she shopped, fully aware of the weather, so as not to take too long. A few freshly baked rolls and a couple of tins of soup, perfect for lunch, she had thought with the icy cold temperatures outside. As she set off back home, she thought it was best that she rang Will to let him know she was on her way, something she had often done whenever she had been out. The plan was that he would have a nice cup of hot chocolate waiting for her, a very much appreciated drink, especially in this cold snap they had been having.

Taking her phone from her bag, she noticed several missed calls from Maurice, although no messages had been left! She had tried a few times to call him back, but with no answer, neither did he return the missed calls, and she had felt a little concerned, especially when the same thing happened when she tried to call Will's phone. Immediately, she began to worry, as her mind suddenly fixated on negative thoughts. Her heart raced, and her pace quickened, as the panic and anxiety kicked in, and as her breathing increased, and her hands began to shake, she could only hope that she would not go into a complete meltdown. Even though her palms were sweaty, and her mouth was dry, she somehow managed to leave a clear voicemail as she headed back home, sharpish. The open fire had been crackling when she returned, and flames of orange licked hungrily at the chimney as they brought a dancing glow into the room. Will was nowhere to be seen, only his father.

Maurice was a tall, smiley, grey-haired man, a true gentleman, one of the kindest, sweetest men that you could ever meet. Even though Eloise and Will had not been married, she had always called him her father-in-law, for she knew she could never have asked for a better one.

With a look of despair upon his face, Eloise was able to tell then, that there was something terribly wrong, even though he had spoken to her in a rather calm tone, considering! He explained that he had arrived at the cottage and found Will collapsed on the bedroom floor, unable to move as if he was paralysed, and that he had tried to help his son to his feet, but failed. Eloise was devastated, but she continued to listen as Maurice explained that he was unsure as to what had happened, but was aware that Will was barely conscious, so he had rung for an ambulance immediately. No one knew how long he had been lying on the floor for, alone and unable to move.

It was the same day that both Eloise and her father-in-law had gone to the hospital, and it had been heartbreaking seeing Will lying there barely aware of what was going on around him. They were told that it was pneumonia, and that he had most likely had it for a length of time, which explained why he kept on feeling unwell. She had kept on saying to him to get checked by the doctor, but like most men, he was very stubborn! Turned out he had a collapsed lung too, which was what most likely caused him to pass out, and Eloise felt shocked and struggled to take in what she had been told, as tears fell from her eyes. She remembered a deep feeling as though she was being suffocated, and a heavy emotion of guilt filled her chest, wishing she hadn't left him that morning. But how was she to know what was going to happen?

The nurse had explained that Will's condition was partly due to the pneumonia, but after further tests, they had found that he had had a stroke too, which was making him generally unwell. She had felt so helpless as she listened to the wheezing sound in his chest with every breath that he took. His pale complexion on his little, distressed face, and the tiredness in his eyes as he faded in and out of consciousness. It had been so painful to watch, and it broke her heart, knowing there had been absolutely nothing she could do for him, all but be by his side, reassuring him he was going to be okay, but even though the specialists had attempted to put lines in several times to feed the necessary medicines, Will in panic mode, had continually pulled them out, although, not aware of what he had been doing. Repeatedly, the staff had attempted to feed the lines back through, but after a few days, he deteriorated even more.

Still certain that he was going to be okay, it was all Eloise could keep telling herself, hoping she was right. But it had been the following day that she was told the words that she had not wanted to hear. That there was nothing more they could do, there had been no more treatments that could help Will get better. The pneumonia itself had gone too far, let alone the stroke, and the medication had not been enough, even though they had tried everything they could possibly try, but nothing had been working. She felt paralysed by the news and asked herself why? Why had they decided to give up? Why had they not found another way to help him? She asked herself repeatedly, How could this have happened. Why had they not been doing more? She had wrestled with the thoughts in her head as a deep pit of despair rumbled in her heart, still not able to process what had happened, nor had she believed what she had been told.

It was the following day that they admitted Will to a nearby hospice and made him as comfortable as possible for his final days, and as hard as it was seeing him that way, Eloise continued to spend all her time with the man she loved, as she told herself he was going to be okay, for she was in denial still. She prayed several times, trying to gain comfort at this difficult time…

'Lord, I ask that you be with Will during this time of need. Please protect him and help him to feel your nearness, knowing that he is not alone, and please give me the strength to get through this difficult time, and protect me from whatever comes my way. Amen.'

It was all Eloise could do: pray. Pray that Will would miraculously make a full recovery. She had always supported him, every step of the way, but she struggled to fight her own battles, too, and it was becoming more difficult for her to stay positive, even though she knew she had to be strong for him.

CHAPTER 2

On the 2nd of September, Eloise had sat with Will all day in the Hospice as she talked about all the places they had been to and what they had done, even though he could not remember any of it. After lunch, the staff had decided to move Will into the room next door, where he could be alone, and she presumed it was because some of the other patients were quite loud and were keeping him awake. Although she had not been too keen on the idea to begin with, however, she knew the staff would have kept a close eye on him, and at least being on his own, he would have peace and quiet. Light streamed through the open window and doors, making the room feel warm and fresh, and despite Will feeling drowsy, he remained awake, eyes wide open, and fought to keep going! Eloise could see he was struggling, really trying so hard to stay awake, yet would not give in, so she felt that the kindest thing to do was to go home and let him get some much-needed rest and go back the following morning to see him. The staff agreed and said they would let her know if there was any change!

As she stepped outside that evening, she shivered from the biting winds that howled, as she cocooned herself within her coat and made her way back to her car. She drove home, grateful for the hot air from her heater, but all she could think about was Will lying in that room alone, hoping that by the time he woke up, he would be feeling a whole lot better! Hope was all she had left to hold on to, and she had to believe that he was going to be okay.

She remembered the night as though it had been yesterday. The fireplace had glowed radiant gold flames, and she had been thankful for the steady heat it brought into the heart of her home, and although her body shivered, the comforting light of the fire soon warmed her up. She had barely been indoors half an hour that evening when her phone rang, and upon answering, she recognised the caller's voice, June, the nurse she had spoken to at the Hospice. Eloise remembered the conversation well.

'Is…Is everything okay? Is Will okay?' She recalled asking with hesitancy and a sorrow-filled voice. June had answered, with, 'I am so sorry, but I have some bad news.' Eloise had swallowed hard; her heart suddenly beat faster as it tightened. 'There is no easy way to say this, but I am so sorry to have to tell you that Will has just passed away.' She could not believe what she had been told, as her blood pulsated through her eardrums, and an overwhelming weight of sadness filled her heart. 'No!' She remembered screaming, as she fell to the floor. 'No, no, no, he can't have.' June had replied with, 'I am so sorry.' Tears then streamed from Eloise's eyes, and her heart moved its way to her throat. She remembered hanging up the phone and screaming.

'Nooooooooooooooooooooooooooooooooooooooo.'

HE … HAS… JUST… PASSED… AWAY.

The words had pierced into her soul, repeatedly, as though her brain had refused to allow any other thought to enter her head, and whilst the words had continued to eat away at her insides, she rocked backwards and forwards on the floor, clutching her breast to keep herself from choking, and with her face in her hands, overwrought with uncontrollable sorrow. She remembered screaming… 'No, no!! Please, No! No.' Nothing could stop the tears, for she felt the most unimaginable pain she had ever experienced in her life. She had sobbed, 'NOOOOOOOOOOOOOOOO.' Overwhelmed and suffocating, her heart was heavy and the pain unbearable, and she had been convinced that she too was dying. She had honestly believed that Will was going to make a full recovery (even though he was in a hospice, and it was the place people go to die, she had not been able to face that fact). None of it made sense! She had not wanted to think for one minute that her love would die! He was her life, and hope had been all she had to keep holding on to and yet, here she was now, facing her life without him.

Maurice had driven Eloise back to the Hospice that evening, as she had not been in a fit state to drive herself. Mikka and Jax, Eloise's two sons, were devastated by the news, but they, too, wanted to say their goodbyes. They had always looked up to Will as a father figure. Jax more so than Mikka, as he was only young when Eloise and Will had first got together. Will had always treated the boys as though they were his own, and they always looked up to him, as sons do to their fathers. She remembered making their silent return, as thoughts swirled around her head, and tears continued to pour from her now blistered eyes. She had bitten her lip so many times that it had swollen, something she had always done when she felt sad and anxious. Maurice seemed somewhat in denial as no tears had fallen from his eyes. Was that shock? Perhaps it was the way he dealt with things, she had thought. Whereas she had not stopped the tears from falling, and her heart felt as though it had broken in two, as if someone had stuck a sharp blade in her and sliced right through.

Once they had arrived at the exterior door to the room that Will was in, where the curtains had been pulled around for privacy, June approached them outside as she hugged Eloise warmly and then Maurice, then Mikka and Jax and extended her sincerest apologies, reassuring them that he went peacefully. 'His eyes just closed and he was gone,' she spoke. 'He must have known!' Eloise had replied. 'That was why he would not go to sleep while I was with him, that is why he kept hanging on. He didn't want me to see him go,' she added. Tears still streamed down her cheeks. 'Perhaps,' replied June. 'But know he is at peace now and no longer suffering.'

Soft music had been playing in the background as they entered through the glass door. Will was there, his hands lying gently across his stomach. He just lay there, as though he were asleep. Eloise never thought she would go from loving Will so hard to seeing him lying still, no longer taking a single breath. The pain had drained from his face, and he just looked at total peace, and as she placed her warm hand in his chilled hand, it was only then, did she believe he had gone. The more she wept, the more her heart had felt like it was going to jump out of her throat, and as she fell to the floor, tears leaked out of her like a dam busting open. She cried… and cried…. and cried. Poor Mikka and Jax had to step back outside, for they had tried so hard to hold back their tears, but sadly, they had no control. It was all just too much for them. Not just seeing their stepfather lying dead, but seeing their mother crying uncontrollably and not having the faintest idea of how they could possibly console her. So much for them to have dealt with, she thought. Why was life so cruel? Maurice had stood for a few seconds, then leaned over and hugged his son as he broke down, and as the tears ran from his eyes, Eloise hugged him, and they both cried in each other's arms. Taking Will's hand in hers once more, she leant and kissed his forehead as she said her goodbyes to the man she loved. She never wanted to leave his side that night; she wanted to stay with him; she wanted to go to where he had gone.

She never thought twice as to what it would feel like to have a loved one taken away from her, in a blink of an eye, yet here she was, alone, feeling totally paralysed. All she kept hearing was, 'he is dead,' piercing through her entire head. Gone were all the plans they had made. She had lost her soulmate…Her best friend… Her rock… Her love… Her life….and Maurice had lost his son.

It was a dark and rainy night when they left the hospice, a piercing gust of wind shook the tree above Eloise's head and showered her already cold frame with a fresh deluge, soaking her hair that hung loosely down her back. After she had said goodbye to her sons, she pulled her coat more closely around her as she quickened her pace back to the car, grateful for her lift home. As she returned to her still, warm cottage, the sky had darkened above. She recalled that a single star had shone brightly that night as she gazed out of her lounge window, and she knew then that it was Will letting her know he was okay. Memories had flooded her head all evening, and pulling one of his shirts from his holdall, she snuggled up to it on the sofa, shortly after she had placed the last couple of logs onto the fire. She watched as it cracked and sparked, sending warmth throughout the room as the sound of the wind whistled down the chimney. The smell of Will was still on the fabric as she buried her nose into it, desperate to hold on to that smell. She remembered talking to him that night, also. 'I am so sorry, my love,' she said out loud, and in her head, he said it was okay, and that there was nothing anyone could have done. 'How am I going to live a life without you?' She said the words to the empty room, knowing he could hear her. 'You were my life. You were my world,' she cried. 'I was supposed to spend the rest of my life with you.' She felt intense sadness as it suddenly hit her that her loved one was gone.

CHAPTER 3

Light beamed through her open blinds, causing
Eloise to stir the following morning, along with the
piercing sound of the alarm going off on her phone.
She had not realised that she had fallen asleep on the
couch the night before, after she wearily collapsed,
still fully dressed, yet here she was with a crook in her
neck and still holding Will's top close to her chest as
she attempted to roll herself onto the floor. She could
not remember the last time she had crashed on her
sofa! Most likely a drunken night out, she thought, a
very long time ago. As she started up the stairs, she
rubbed the sleep out of her eyes and ran her fingers
through her tangled hair, and headed to the bathroom
to take a shower, ready to try and face another day.
She had not felt much like getting dressed; in fact, she
had barely felt much like doing anything, having little
motivation in herself. The next few days had been a
total blur for Eloise, as one thing blended into another,
having all the legal side of things to sort out and close
friends of Will's to have to break the news to. Some
closer than others, and she knew it would be a total
shock to a lot of them. Then there was the chapel of
rest she needed to get in touch with, and the minister
at the crematorium, to be able to discuss the funeral. It
had been something Will had always made perfectly
clear: that he may not have been a very religious man,
but he had been adamant that he wanted to be

cremated, and that was okay. She wanted to make sure that he was to have the best send-off that he so deserved.

It was midday before she had met up with Maurice at the funeral parlour, they were greeted by a lovely lady by the name of Rachel. Dressed smartly in her black skirt and jacket, she directed them into a room which had an elegant feel to it, like a calming oasis. A dark wooden table stood in the centre, and a glass cabinet in the far corner, which held a variety of different coloured urns, which immediately caught her eye. Grateful to the friendly warmth of the lady, her guidance and help that had been provided had been comforting at such a difficult time, and after they had talked for ages defining what they wanted on the day of Wills funeral, Eloise had decided on a small heart urn from the cabinet that she had spotted earlier, and stated that she would like some of Wills ashes to keep with her. She picked out a red heart as it felt the appropriate colour to have for the love they had for one another.

The rain outside had turned into a nasty sleet, and Eloise was grateful that her car was parked just across the road from the chapel of rest. She bid farewell to Maurice and, whilst struggling with her emotions, attempted the drive to where some of Will's ashes were to be scattered after his funeral. The ground was quite icy from the sleet that had built up, making the roads quite slippery, and she was aware that some people were driving like idiots, unlike herself, who took things steadily so as not to have any accidents. Thankfully, the crematorium was barely ten minutes away. Grateful that she had dressed reasonably suitable in two pairs of socks, a heavy pullover with a thick pair of jeans and a bright pink padded coat that came down to her ankles with matching pink boots, meant that she was well protected even though she could instantly feel the cold wind enter her soul, as she stepped out of her car, almost taking her breath away. She did not care what she looked like as long as she was warm, even if she did get strange looks from each passerby. The entire ground was coated in a blanket of slush as the trees shivered in the bitter wind, their branches naked and their leaves bejewelled with frost. Out of nowhere, a pure white feather dropped down by Eloise's side, and she knew then that Will was close by. She stood for a while, thinking of him and how much her life was going to be so different without him in it, trying to think of ways in which to keep him close still. There was no doubt that she was struggling without him, and that no matter how much people had tried to tell her it would get easier, she tried to say that it was more about not wanting to live without him. She hurt so bad, there was a heavy feeling in her chest where she could not speak or move, a wish to close her eyes and not wake up, because the pain, her broken heart, was exhausting. She had lost her whole world. Every kiss they ever shared, every hand she had ever held, every smile he had given her, every moment of love. Every laugh, every minute of togetherness. She had lost it all. She just wanted him to hold her and say: 'I've got you.'

The weather had begun to take a turn for the worse as snow fell from the shackle grey sky, and Eloise shivered in the bitter wind as clusters of twigs fell from the branches above her. She left rather swiftly so as not to get caught in the massive downpour of the blasting snowstorm, and as the cold night closed in around her, she was grateful for the logs she had put on her fire before she had gone out. The flickers of light bounced off each log as a display of warm hues danced amongst each flame, capturing the essence of beauty that filled the room. As nighttime drew in, Eloise was grateful to be able to collapse in a heap after such a draining day, as she pulled her best nightdress over her weary head, slid back the light quilt, and almost fell into her inviting bed. She knew she had so much to contend with over the coming weeks, and believed that the rest of her life was going to be full of sadness as she lay in bed trying to understand why Will had to go, and as her eyes welled up, it suddenly hit her, that she was never going to hear his voice again, or see his smile. He was not coming back.

CHAPTER 4

It was the 14th of October, the day of the funeral. One of the worst days Eloise had ever had to face in her whole life. With a heavy heart, she looked out of the window to a dark and dismal day, with its grey hues and rain-filled clouds. She had spent far too long in the shower, her head down, trying to muster up the strength for her day ahead. Deep down, she had hoped the water would wash away her tension as she wiped away the tears from her eyes and emerged in a cloud of steam with her pale skin and fingers wrinkled like prunes. Her outfit hung over the bedroom door, so as not to crease, whilst she ran the hairdryer through her long, wet hair. It had taken less than fifteen minutes to get dressed, as she stood before her full-length mirror, hating the reflection that stared back at her. Gone were her curves in all the right places that she had once been proud of. Gone was the sparkle in her eyes that once lit up her face. One last quick glance in the hall mirror and she was ready. Well, ready as she would ever be! Both Eloise's sons, Mikka and Jax and Wills' Dad Maurice, were dressed smartly in their black shirts, each wearing a red tie to complete the look. As the hearse pulled up outside the cottage, she stood by it for a moment, trying to gather her thoughts for the day ahead, and as she blew a kiss to Will, the tears ran down her mournful face.

Rachel, being the chief mourner, walked slowly in front of the hearse for a short distance, whilst all the villagers stood in a line to mark their respects for the man they all loved, and as she reached the end of the road, she then climbed back into the hearse as the rest followed behind in their cars. A steady drizzle of rain began to descend from sombre clouds as they continued their journey ahead, and once they had arrived at the crematorium, Eloise knew that moment had come. Her time to say goodbye. As Maurice took her hand, she tried to hold her emotions as her head filled with a dark fog, but she knew it would not be long before she would break. Everything felt different; in fact, nothing felt real because she was feeling so numb, surrounded by all these people-people that she had never even seen before, and it was at that moment that she completely lost all that was going on around her as tears fell from her eyes, drenching the tissues she had in her hand. She took to her seat, and the minister began the service with his welcoming and opening words and then read out the tribute to Will, written by Maurice, and although his soft, gentle voice was calming, Eloise still managed to cry throughout. It was then her turn, as she took to the stand to read out her Eulogy, and as she stopped for a second, she just stared at the coffin that stood at the side of her, knowing she would no longer be able to see or feel or touch Will, no longer would she feel his kisses upon her lips, feel his tender touch, have him hold her in her arms and tell her he loved her, and as she composed herself for a second, she continued to read in between the tears, as she read out the last line of her tribute to the man she loved:

'Our time may be no longer, but the love we had for each other will always be with us, and until we are once again together, my love, I will no longer be complete. I am merely here, waiting my turn.'

The closing music followed shortly after, and as the curtain pulled slowly around the coffin, Eloise emerged from the chapel, feeling as if she was suddenly paralysed, like she was suffocating, as if a giant hand was clamped around her heart. Deep realisation swept through her, in sharp waves of pain, and her heart pounded in her chest slowly, as her legs began to tremble, and she fell to her knees. With her head in her hands, she cried uncontrollably to the point where she thought she would never stop. It had been the longest and most emotionally exhausting time of Eloise's life, and things never got any easier. Most days were spent in her PJs, crying, wishing Will was still with her, as memories of him flooded her mind, her shallow breath, her pounding heart, and the cry of sorrow drowned her brain. She always felt cold and alone, and every day that she woke, she would kiss the photo of him that was sat at her bedside, and every evening before going to sleep, she would talk to him and tell him about her day and how much she was missing him, before giving his photo a goodnight kiss. Her journal was written in daily, but it never got any easier; in fact, every day that she was without him, she struggled increasingly, because everywhere seemed so quiet and nothing felt real anymore. Although her family had been amazing and a great support, she still felt so lost without her beloved in her life. Maurice had been her rock through all that she had been through in her grieving journey, and so had her mum, and she was truly grateful to them both, but living so far away, it was not always easy to see them, especially with the way the weather had been as of lately. However, when they did meet up, they always talked about Will and on the odd occasion, Eloise even managed a smile.

With the cold weather outside and the snow still coming down heavily, it did not really give her any inclination to want to go out, even though she desperately needed some essentials. She had run out of everything indoors, and the cupboards were beginning to look a little sorry for themselves. The two microwave meals she had left in the freezer would have to be sufficient for the time being she thought, until she was able to force herself into the real world again, but at the moment, she could not face going to all the places her and Will used to go to or face anyone, having to talk to people or answer their questions to how she was feeling, it was all just too much…. too soon.

Eloise Darlington had always come across as a happy, smiley person, but a lot of the time that was an act when she was in front of others. Always one to pretend that she was okay, this happy, go-lucky woman who never liked to give anything away! Maybe that is why no one ever knew about all her problems. She was good at hiding things and certainly never talked about anything to anyone, not even her family. She had never been the kind of person who felt she had to burden everyone with her thoughts and feelings and did not want to worry any members of her family, so it was easier for her to keep it all to herself. She was never even able to confide in a friend, as she did not really have any that lived close by. Well, there was one, but she was never interested in what Eloise had to say for herself, it was always about her, and as soon as she even began to start telling her about how she felt, or any worries she had, she would just talk over her and change the subject, so she stopped saying anything, she never bothered to share anything with her anymore. In fact, she had not even heard from her in a very long time. However, she did have one good friend with whom she had stayed in touch with since school. Greta was her name. Oh, what a lovely woman she was. A short lady, who often had a few streaks of colour combed through her silver hair, usually blue, and although they did not live close to one another, they always kept in touch and met up whenever they possibly could. She was good for Eloise, with her bubbly character and always smiling and laughing, she always knew how to cheer her up, and besides living some distance apart, they always kept in touch by phone and messaging. Even if it had been ages since they had even spoken a word, when they did finally catch up again, it was as if they had never been away from one another. Greta had been through a lot of trauma in her lifetime, what with losing her dear mum and dad and then her wonderful husband. Marty was so good for Greta as he truly cared and loved her so much; he always looked out for her and put her first. When he passed, very suddenly, it broke Gretas' heart and Eloise, although she tried so hard to be there for her, she so wished she could have done so much more, and she knew too, that it would break Gretas' heart if she were to see her best friend letting herself go.

With her long mousy brown hair, normally styled beautifully, and her skin as smooth as silk, Eloise always looked so natural and pretty without having to make any fuss, and Greta always complimented her on her looks. Her big brown eyes always sparkled, and her gentle smile was always the trait that Will loved about her. It was one of the first things that drew her to him and made him fall in love with her, and she knew that he would hate to see her with such sad eyes and no smile since he had passed away. She had let herself go, for she did not feel the need to look good anymore, felt she had no reason to. Just getting up in the morning was an effort, and she had not even gone to work in what felt like forever, because she could not face it, although Eloise was grateful to her company for letting her have a break at such a difficult time.

CHAPTER 5

It had been twelve weeks since Will had slipped away, and even though Eloise knew he was at peace now and knew he was with his mum, it did not make it any easier for her. It did not stop her from missing him every single moment of every day, as she tried to face each day without him, and she often wondered how Maurice coped. The last time she had spoken to him, he was quite poorly himself, although not surprisingly, as he had not only lost his son but also his beloved wife had passed away just a couple of years before. It was enough to take its toll on anyone's body.

Mary Devoir was the most-kindest, sweetest lady you could ever meet, who had a heart of gold and would do anything for anyone. A beautiful woman with a beautiful soul, whose smile lit up the room. Like a mum to Eloise, she was always there for her, and they had spent many a time having heart-to-hearts. Sadly, when she passed away, Will had found it so difficult not having her in his life, but Eloise knew that she would be looking after him now, and she felt grateful for that, but it did not stop her from wanting to be with him. She had visited the crematorium daily after the remaining ashes of his had been scattered. The beautiful, serene garden of remembrance had become her sanctuary, nestled in a beautiful and peaceful natural woodland setting. It was a place of peace for her, and she was sure it had been to many others, too. With its fifteen acres of ground, it was home to wild deer and a variety of shrubs, trees, and plants. It was also home to a beautiful Daisy Garden, a tranquil place where families could remember their own baby in peace and have the comfort that their babies were not alone. Eloise visited the crematorium every day after Will had passed away and knew that when it was to come to the summer and autumn, they would be the prettiest seasons, as she visited Mary often. In the summer, the woods would always be filled with a kaleidoscope of colour, as the sweet smell of honeysuckle filled the air, and she would enjoy a walk under the dappled, cool shade of the trees and watch the butterflies glide from flower to flower and listen to the birds singing sweetly in the branches as the robins came to sit gently at her side, and as the autumn slowly weaved its way in, the molten red leaves would blow from the trees, and lay like a blanket on the ground. Eloise liked the way they crunched under her feet as she took each step, but this time of year, it was not as nice, as the wind bustled through the branches of the trees, and leaves sat half embedded into the dark and damp ground, which was wet from the sleet. Rustling sounds of small animals were quite often heard, as they scurried under the thick ferns, and over the many brittle twigs and broken branches that had been blown down previously from the high winds.

The car park had been empty, which made a change, as all too often Eloise had arrived just as a coffin was about to be taken out from the back of a hearse, which had always been a sad thing to see. Many a time she had turned up to a stunning glass-fronted carriage with beautiful white horses, a graceful and elegant final salute, so Eloise had thought. How lovely to have one's final journey in such a testament of beauty and peace.

Inhaling the fresh air as the breeze whipped her hair across her face, and grateful for her thick woolly jumper she had put on underneath her teddy coat, she placed Will's favourite red roses down by his tree. 'There you go, my love,' she whispered. 'Your favourites.' The icy wind whistled through the thin branches of the bare trees, and as she stood back from the flowers, she wrapped herself tightly in her coat to try to shield herself from the bitter weather. There had often been other people around, whether it be walking the beautiful grounds, or just sitting by their loved ones chatting away, and on the odd occasion, there would be the ones that would nod to Eloise as they passed by her, sometimes she would even get the odd hello. Most of the time, she just sat and cried her heart out, but quite often, she liked to just sit and gather her thoughts. Today had been one of those moments where she wanted a conversation with Will, and if it had been anywhere else, she would probably have been certified as crazy for talking to him the way she did here, but this was something she had done since the day he had passed away, and she believed he could hear every single word she spoke.

As she stood beneath the huge oak tree that sheltered her from the wind and rain, she broke down to him. 'I miss you,' she cried. 'Since the day you left, there has been an emptiness in my heart,' she continued. 'I wish so much that you could be here. I know that you are up there watching me, and I know you are in a beautiful place,' she lifted her head and pushed back a layer of hair and tucked it neatly behind her ear, as tears slowly trickled down her sullen cheeks. 'I know you are in a place full of love, and compassion, and all things incredible,' she went on. 'But I so wish you were here with me.' Reaching into her coat pocket for a tissue, she gently wiped her tear-stained eyes. 'Just look at me,' she uttered. 'What an emotional wreck I am.' Gently placing the tissue back into her pocket, she gracefully rearranged his red roses by the tree. 'You know you will always be in my heart, my sweet love, and I will cherish every memory of you until we meet in heaven.'

Eloise had always been so grateful for her faith, knowing that Will was in heaven and no longer suffering, but although she believed that she would be with him again one day, having to try and live in the here and now was becoming increasingly impossible for her as she was hurting more as each day passed. Since his death, she had hit a downward spiral, going from grief into a massive dark hole, with no real motivation. Her life had reached a turmoil where she had come to a point of giving up completely, and feared she would never resurface. Even though she had continued to suffer in silence, she eventually took some advice from her dear friend and promised to seek help, as she thought back to her sessions with her Bereavement Counsellor, recalling that most of the 45 minutes with her had been spent crying. As she had sat in a corner of the scarcely furnished room, and Sonia, the counsellor, having very little to say, the time had gone, and Eloise had barely put two sentences together. She always seemed to ask the same questions, too, and Eloise had been tired of continuously repeating herself each week. 'So, Eloise, what have you done this last week?' Sonia would ask. 'Nothing. I do not want to do anything,' she cried, staring at the floor. Sonia had paused; in hope Eloise may have followed on with something else. 'How are you sleeping?' 'I'm not,' Eloise replied. 'I cannot sleep, for every time I close my eyes, I keep replaying my last moments with Will.' She clenched her fists tightly into her lap. Tears spilled down her cheeks as she tried to speak. 'I do not want to be here anymore; I keep telling you, I want to be with Will.' 'But you are still here, Eloise,' Sonia had said with a smile. 'Try to think of something positive that you have in your life. What might that be?' Eloise had raised her head to look at Sonia as tears spilt down her sullen face once more. Well, that was an obvious answer, so she had thought! 'My family, and my boys.' 'Okay, that's good,' Sonia had replied. 'So maybe try to focus on your family as a positive, every time you have a moment of feeling low.' Eloise had nodded as she wiped the tears from her eyes. Eight weeks she had gone to the sessions and not one of them had made the slightest difference, and now here she was, still feeling the same. No matter how many times family or friends or bereavement counsellors had said to her that there was nothing she could have done to save Will, it still had not made any difference to how Eloise was feeling. She had lost count of the number of people who had continued to tell her to move on and to get over it. These had only made her worse; in fact, they had put a barrier up in front of her, so she did not have to acknowledge any of the things that were being said. No one knew what she was going through or the pain she was feeling. Eloise did not even know who she was anymore and hated this feeling of loneliness, ripping out her heart and tearing away at her soul, feeling lost and confused. Memories of the many happy times she had shared with Will crossed her mind, and as the thoughts kept coming, she could not help but feel intense sadness, as tears continued to roll down her cheeks, as the thoughts turned once again to her wanting to end her life.

What choice did she have? Most would be likely to say that she was being selfish, and wondering why, and how could she possibly have these thoughts, when she had loved ones that cared about her so much, and as the bereavement counsellor had kept on saying, her mum, her sons, and Maurice. Had she ever stopped to think about them? Of course, she had. She had never once stopped thinking about them, and what this would do to them, and the fact she had her faith too, how could she even possibly think of talking in this way! But, this feeling of heartache was eating away inside her, it was all just too much for her to go on living and oh, how sorry she was that she could never tell anyone how her soul was so broken, but she could no longer live in her world of pain with the suffering she faced every day, she could not be without him anymore. The man she loved.

As Eloise blew a kiss in the air to Will, she headed back to her car, grateful for the shelter from the rain on this cold, wet and windy day. Luckily, it had only been a short car ride home, and she was thankful for the warmth that came from her log fire as she entered her cosy cottage, and once again, the unbearable reality hit her right there- her love had truly been taken away from her. She had tried repeatedly to overcome this heartbreaking feeling, but the tears continued to come thick and fast as she was continuously reminded that her man had gone! Her empty home, with its unfilled place beside her in bed, waking up alone, instead of snuggling up into his naked body. Now all she had was an empty space, the space he used to fill.

As a lump formed in her throat, images of Will played in her mind once again. She closed her eyes and inhaled a shaking breath, as her mind wandered. 'Oh, Will, I wish you were here to wrap me up in your arms.' Tears escaped as they rolled gently down her cheeks, as she held tightly on to his photo close to her chest, eying up the pills that sat on her nearside cabinet. She had thought about taking them many a time, just a few to mask the pain she had been feeling and to help her sleep, but this was different; she did not want to just sleep for a few hours!

She had written letters to each one of her family members just a few weeks previous, when she very first had thoughts of ending her life, but nothing became of it then, as she tried to believe that she would be able to cope better and try to find a way to slowly move forward, so she hid the letters away. People were always telling her that it gets better with time and that she will move on, but she just wanted to scream at them until she had no voice left, and who were they to tell her that she would move on!! She did not want to move on; she did not want to be without him. He was the love of her life; the man she wanted to spend the rest of her life with. She understood that people meant well, but what they were saying was not what Eloise wanted to hear. To be honest, she would rather they say nothing and just let her deal with it in her own way.

Maybe it was why she always kept her feelings to herself…

Why she never let anyone see her cry…

Why she was always smiling on the outside, yet dying on the inside, because deep down, she was trying to hide it all away. It was why she kept on pretending she was okay, so they did not keep on asking the same questions. She was just trying to deal with the situation the only way she knew how to… in the only way that made sense to her, but as she continued to struggle, her life never got any easier, even though this was not a spur of the moment decision, rather something she had been thinking about for some time now, she knew that now was the right time. She had kept the letters simple, not really thinking about exactly what was going to happen back then or how it was to happen, as she did not have anything rehearsed or laid out, but now, here she was, knowing precisely what she wanted and knowing it was the right thing to do.

The letters read:

It is with a heavy heart that I write you this letter, knowing the amount of pain it is going to cause you. I know that by the time you get to read this, I will be gone. I want you to remember that I love you so much, and I know this is the cruellest thing I could possibly do to hurt you, and I am so sorry, but I am hurting so, so much that it is eating away at me beyond my control. Please, please do not ever think for one minute that I do not care about you or love you, because I do, very much so. I have tried so hard since Will left this life, and I simply cannot carry on without him. I miss him so much. I know it is very selfish of me, but I hope one day you will forgive me. I love you more than you could ever possibly know. Do not ever forget that.

Love you always x

Eloise knew deep down it was not the right thing to do considering her faith, but she believed that there was no other way to stop this feeling. She wanted to sleep and never wake up. She wanted God to take her, to let her be with Will. She reached for her pill bottle and tipped out the contents beside her as tears streamed down her sullen face. There was only one way she could go, to end her forever pain, as she swallowed one by one…. Not thinking of the consequences but just wanting to be with her beloved once again. Her lids started to feel heavy as she began to think about Will once more, and throwing the empty pill bottle onto the floor and leaving the letters on the bedside cabinet, she slowly drifted off to sleep.

CHAPTER 6

Eloise could scarcely recall being in the ambulance, only remembering the noise of the siren, although, due to the weather conditions, it was not going as fast as it would normally go in an emergency. She had no idea who even called it, as she was in and out of consciousness and slowly deteriorating by the minute, and by the time she had reached the hospital, things took a turn for the worse. The medical team were at her bedside regularly checking to see if there were any signs of movement or any signs of response, but nothing.

Six weeks passed, and she was still hooked up to the breathing machine in intensive care, still fighting for her life after taking the overdose. Visitors came and went, but there was no change, and it was unlikely that anything would happen anytime soon; neither was there anything else the staff could do. It was just a matter of waiting to see whether she would wake up by herself, hoping she would open her eyes. It was during the middle of the night, whilst lying in her hospital bed, that a bright light appeared before Eloise, and by some miracle, she awakened. Two figures dressed in long white robes that hung well below their feet, with gold belts tied loosely around their waists, were vaguely visible. Eloise could not quite make out their faces as they were partly covered by hoods, but the skin that she could see was like pure porcelain, and any hair that they might have had was hidden. Not a word was spoken, as they floated above the floor, but it did not freak Eloise out, although she was not sure anymore if she was dreaming or if she was being welcomed by what she could only imagine as 'angels,' well, that was what she could only assume, being angels was the only possible explanation! Although whenever she had ever tried to picture angels in her head, she had always believed that they would have wings! But isn't that what anyone would imagine, and that they would be suddenly whisked off! But these angels, these angels were gentle, incredibly warm, and friendly as they carefully unhooked her from every wire and tube she was attached to. In fact, she was reasonably calm as they raised her off her bed with gentleness and ease, and she knew in that moment that she did not need to feel afraid, but instead, to feel great comfort. Just at that moment, an unexplainable light that let off the most beautiful aura of pureness engulfed her existence as they carried her towards it. Where were they taking her? She thought, as she felt a sense of calmness surround her as a blinding light swept around her feet, then upwards, washing away all the weariness that she had through her entire body. Being shrouded in this light finally brought her to believe that she was no longer alive because she felt free and no longer in any pain, but as she was being carried away, she could not help but look back several times. As they moved on a little further, then stopped again, she turned around once more, and out of nowhere, all her loved ones had appeared, and were stood crying like they knew what was happening. Could they really have been here? She thought! Her sons begged her not to leave, as they tried to reach her, but she kept on drifting further away. Her mum stood there too, stretching her arms out, desperate to hold on to her daughter, and her sisters fought to pull her back, but Eloise was getting further away until she was out of complete reach. She knew that there was nothing more either of them or she could do.

A gliding, gentle sensation continued as she floated in mid-air, unaware of what was really happening, apart from the fact that it was so beautiful, serene, and calm that she did not want it to end ever, as her body continued to float gently into the undulating beauty that lay stretched before her eyes. Although it was the most stunning sight she had ever seen, she was uncertain at the time of how long it took her on her journey, because she was not sure if time even existed! As she continued into the heavenly light ahead, although being brighter than the sun, it did not hurt her eyes to look at it, and once she reached the end, the angels disappeared and she never saw them again, but what she did see, hear and feel were things beyond her imagination! Two huge golden gates stood before her, and it was then that she realised where she was, as she suddenly became aware of a figure standing by the gate. A tall man with white hair and a bushy white beard. 'This must be Peter,' she said out loud to herself. His look was of warmth, well, that was how he came across as, so she thought. 'Saint Peter, he holds the key to heaven.' That much she knew. With broad shoulders and a circular face, his solid frame stood tall, approximately five feet ten inches, whilst his dark eyes, which had a blue tint to them, lit up his lovely smile. Eloise had no idea what she expected him to look like, and although his clothes looked as though they had been worn for years, and his dark grey robe hung loosely, as though it was ten times too big for him, he looked dapper. He seemed a gentle man, and even though he towered over Eloise, he came across as a warm and kind figure. His huge hands took hold of the book, which sat neatly on a lectern directly in front of him, the craftsmanship of which was expertly constructed, as he opened it with care. The 'Book of Life,' she thought to herself, and knew that it was the book in which God records the names of every person who is appointed to heaven, and she understood then that she would not be going any further. This had to be a dream, for she knew how this worked, and that they would not allow her to enter heaven, not yet anyway. Peter directed his attention to a page in the book like he knew exactly where to turn and ran his finger down the side of the sheet of paper. As he closed the book with gentleness, Eloise knew then, that was it. This was where she had to turn around and go back, but much to her surprise, Peter opened the heavy gate in front of her, and she knew then that her name must have been on the list, which could only mean one thing! She had died. This was not a dream like she had first imagined.

'You will learn many things about yourself once you go through the gates,' stated Peter. 'Any sin will be completely removed,' he added. Eloise was grateful for what she was being told by this glorious man. 'You will learn so much about yourself, and you will meet family, friends, and loved ones. There will be no pain, no negativity, and you shall not be hurt in any way,' he continued. As Peter pushed open the gate to allow her to enter, Eloise discovered that she was suddenly wearing all white! Looking herself up and down, feeling puzzled as to why? 'The emphasis on this,' stated Peter, 'is that the white relates to you being clean. The white robe shows purity. You may go on in now,' he nodded, and Eloise smiled, accepting his approval.

As she entered the gates, she was filled with a sense of anticipation and was immediately struck by the beauty of what lay in front of her, for it was beyond anything imaginable on earth. Dazzling hues stretched as far as the eye could see, and pathways of individual bricks of gold lay stretched in front of her feet, as white roses cascaded their petals on the ground where everyone walked, as the sound of organs played in tune, and voices of angels sang around her in the most beautiful harmonies. Heaven was a symphony of music, filled with perfectly pitched voices, not a single one off-key, and it was the most beautiful sound Eloise had ever heard, and impossible to feel anything other than sheer tranquillity. She had stepped into another world. A world so stunning, so peaceful, that she was happy to be where she was, and knew straight away that she was in the presence of God, and not just aware of him, but felt him too, as the closeness of him overwhelmed her with love. Before Eloise entered heaven, she had often thought about all the questions she would want to ask God when her time had come, and yet, here she was now, in this beautiful place of his, yet all the questions she had for him no longer needed answers.

As a figure slowly approached her, she immediately knew it was Will, as her heart skipped a beat. A magnificent sight to see, she thought, as he stood before her now, gorgeous, clean-shaven and looking rather dapper in his white robe of fine linen. His eyes caught hers as they exchanged smiles, and they both just stood and stared at one another, rather like the first time they met. As Will lifted his right hand, he motioned Eloise over towards him and into his arms. 'My Queen,' he whispered. Just as he had always called her. 'At last,' she replied. 'I have waited so long to be with you again.' Will took her hand in his, raised it to his lips, and kissed it gently as she looked up at him with a smile. 'I am so happy that I am right by your side, Will.' 'Me too, my love,' he replied, as he leaned forward and kissed her again. It felt good to see his gorgeous face and comforting to be in the warmth of his body once more. His smile, which came from deep within him, illuminated every part of where Eloise stood like a sudden beam of light, and it was at that moment that her heart filled with joy as he held her tight. She felt loved. More loved than she had ever felt before, and she knew then that she was home. She was where she belonged.

Eloise had no idea what lay ahead, but she sensed that with each step she would take next, it would be increasingly beautiful. As Will placed his hand in hers, he gently pulled her close to his side. 'Come with me,' he said. 'I have so much to show you and so many people for you to see.' He squeezed her hand gently and led the way. 'I cannot wait,' she responded with excitement. The air was still, and she felt as if it was embracing her as she walked. 'This place is breathtaking, I have never seen anything so exquisite,' she added, taking in all the glorious wonder of all that flowed around her. Everywhere was full of love and colour, a sanctuary where nature filled every space, whilst a softness was felt beneath her feet as she walked. 'It is a place of endless joy and love,' replied Will with a smile. Eloise was amazed at all that she witnessed, as she continued to explore beautiful heaven. All around her were people of all ages and nationalities, some in groups and some just on their own, and she could not help but notice how many of those people had children with them and how happy and well they all looked. All those that she met were kind and welcoming as they talked about their lives in heaven, sharing stories of hope and love. Their clothes were of fine, bright linen, white and pure as the snow and fitted perfectly to every individual one, and all around looked so clean, the scenery as striking as paradise, with lush gardens and beautiful parks filling every space, whilst the scent of fresh flowers burst throughout the air. It was a world Eloise had never imagined could be so beautiful, with countless footpaths going in various directions, and she was intrigued to find out where they all led to! 'Will, where are you taking me?' She asked, as the warm air enveloped her, casting its radiant glow over everything in its path. 'Home,' my love, he answered tenderly.' Home?' She questioned, unaware that they would have a house here, although, beaming with excitement, she was sure the house would be something of perfection, going by all the beauty she had seen so far on their walk. 'Yes, I have been working on it since I came here to make it special for when you arrived,' Will smiled. 'With some help from God, of course,' he added. 'Come, I shall show you.'

As a brightness cast a rosy hue across the afternoon heavenly space, golden fingers of light lit up the scene as they drifted lazily in the gentle breeze. As they walked a short distance further, Eloise was mesmerised by the beauty that surrounded her and the sweet, sap smell that hung in the air. All through the grounds as they walked, were magnificent houses everywhere, with golden pathways leading up to the front doors and grounds adjoining the houses with beautiful trees, bearing every fruit you could possibly want, and she could not believe all the grandeur that surrounded her and how it filled so much space. Whoever knew that heaven was such an enormous place?

CHAPTER 7

Walking at a leisurely pace, they eventually came to a huge, shingled path, more like a driveway, Eloise thought. It was surrounded by white orchid trees, their trunks giving rise to numerous slender branches, as a dappled light shone through them. They danced in the breeze, casting shadows onto the yellow stone of shingle, and she was transfixed by them as they stood tall, parallel to the house, the most stunning house she had ever set her eyes upon. 'This is our home,' Will announced. 'This one right here,' he pointed. 'It is called Whispering Pines.' It was more like a mansion, Eloise thought, with its white marble wall cladding that stood out for its brightness and elegance, not forgetting its durability. She stood transfixed at the stunning beauty that lay in front of her, for she had never seen anything so beautiful, so clean, so white, so pure. 'This?' She hesitated for a second. 'This is really our home?' She asked Will, surprised. 'Yes,' he replied. 'It is all ours.'

Just before Eloise entered her home, a recognisable woman greeted her, her deep-set eyes shimmered with such a familiarity. 'Hello, I am sure you don't remember me, I am Rosie, an old friend of your parents,' she said. Her voice was soft and gentle, and it stirred something within Eloise. 'Yes, yes, I remember you, you used to live next door, am I right?' 'That is right, my dear. You were a wee child

back then,' she cried as she gave Eloise a warm
embrace. 'Yes, you used to have a dog called Jake,'
Eloise added, remembering the black Labrador that
was so, so friendly. She could not believe how healthy
Rosie looked, her complexion so smooth! 'I do
apologise, but I have only just arrived here, and Will
is about to show me our home. Can we catch up
another time?' 'Yes, of course, my dear, I shall look
forward to that.' Rosie dropped a sweet smile, and
there was a warm hug between the two of them as
they parted ways.

Nothing could prepare Eloise for the moment she
was about to experience, for she had no idea what to
expect!

The white marble abode stood on a plot of its own,
with its enormously wooden door carved in walnut, as
flowers weaved amongst the trellising that was
secured to each of the pillars at either side of the
building. Fruit trees covered every inch of space
alongside of this beautiful house, from Plum trees to
peaches, Mangos to Pears, Apricots to Apples. She
had never seen so many fruit trees all in one place.
'Can I go inside?' She asked eagerly. Her eyes lit up
as a rush of excitement sent colour to her cheeks, as
she tore her gaze from Will, focusing her attention on
the house. 'Of course, my love,' replied Will, as he
pushed the heavy door open. Upon entering the house,
she was struck by a mesmerising smell of Lilies that
filled the hallway and was blown away by the beauty
that filled the space in front of her, like nothing she

had ever seen before. A grand staircase of yellow marble, with its wrought iron and gilt bronze railing, stood boldly in the centre of the hall, and her first thought being, this was like something from a fairy-tale, a house that you could only possibly dream of, and as tears welled up in her eyes, she suddenly felt overwhelmed, as she realised how real this all was. This was her house. Hers and Will's home, where they could finally be together again, never again to be apart. It was all that she wanted, all she had thought about since he had first passed away. This was the most beautiful of houses that she had ever set her eyes on, filled with elegance and charm, and yet, she had only just stepped into the first room. A huge lamp that had been sculptured with angelic figures from its top to its bottom, stood in the far corner. 'I had that especially made for you,' Will announced. 'The angelic figures symbolise protection and blessing.' 'It is absolutely beautiful,' Eloise replied. 'Truly unique.' She was captivated by the detail that had gone into designing the magnificent piece of art that stood in front of her, but also touched that Will had made such a determined attempt of achieving such a beautiful piece.

The lounge was to the left of the extremely impressive entrance hall, and Eloise was overwhelmed at the sheer beauty that this stunning room gave out as she entered it, amazed at the way in which Will had kept with the stunning yellows that flowed through into this room. Decorative gold leaf crystal lights and mirrors hung gracefully in this exquisite space, whilst the walls, which were covered with an intricate cream fabric, brought out the yellow silk cut velvet upholstery of the appealing sofas that stood in the centre of the room. Elegant yellow velvet drapes framed the beautiful arched windows, whilst lace inner curtains remained drawn, allowing the light to enter whilst rendering the heart-stopping view from outside. 'Is this gorgeous place really mine?' She asked Will, once more, as her emotions filled up inside her. 'Yes, my love,' he replied. 'It is your home. Our home.'

From the heavenly lounge, into the charming dining room, Eloise was once again moved by the elegance that continued to flow, and the room itself was big enough to hold several people in, if ever she wished to throw a huge dinner party. Six chairs stood, gilded with bronze paint and yellow velvet covers to again match the rest of the upholstery, and were remarkably stunning, and the solid table, also gilded with bronze paint, was pleasing to the eye, in which Eloise was sure would last forever. The kitchen was the heart of the home, a modern, stylish room with its blend of functionality, designed to be both a workspace and a place of sheer comfort. Fitted cupboards and stunning black marble work surfaces reflected the light and added a touch of elegance, as well as being incredibly spacious. The whole of the downstairs had ceramic flooring. 'Easier to clean,' Eloise stated, content with the choice Will had made. 'I am absolutely moved by how beautiful you have made this look, Will,' she smiled. 'Who would have thought that you could design such a stunning look of beauty! Did you do all the work yourself?' 'No, I had a little help, but mainly with the painting, marble work and the fitting of the kitchen.' 'Well, it is simply stunning.' 'I had an idea on colour as I knew yellow was one of your favourites, although the interior designing was down to my mother,' Will added. 'Bless her,' Eloise smiled. 'She has done an amazing job. I must thank her.'

Mary Devoir had always had a good eye for detail, and like Eloise, she knew what colours and styles matched and had a pretty good idea of what Eloise would have liked in her home. Between her and Will, they had done an amazing job, and Eloise was overcome with emotion at the extent and elegance of this exquisite abode, which she now called home. 'I will take you to see her,' answered Will, as he continued to show his love the rest of the house. 'There are so many wonderful people you will get to meet here,' he promised. 'Some that you haven't seen for a while.'

It was a considerable amount of time that Eloise spent in her delightful dwelling, and she was so overwhelmed by all that she had seen so far since she had arrived in this graceful place that she was beginning to feel more at home and getting used to her beautiful heavenly life. 'You must rest now, my love,' insisted Will. 'There is so much more I need to show you, and so many things for you to learn, but you need to get some rest first. Eloise was sure he was right and looked forward to meeting all the wonderful people who had come to Heaven before her.

CHAPTER 8

As glittering sunrays spread hues of silvers and golds and the light danced through the gap in the drapes, Eloise had been charmed by all that she had seen and grateful for her rest. She had slept peacefully and was excited to see what else Will had planned to show her in this heavenly place and what she might learn! She was looking forward to seeing people that had meant so much to her before they had died, some that she had not seen for many years. 'I would like to take you to see my mother as promised,' said Will. He knew she would be one of the people that Eloise would want to see again. 'Oh yes,' she answered eagerly.

It had been several years since Mary Devoir had passed away. She had been quite poorly for some time, and it was devastating, the day she was taken, for it was so sudden, and heartbreaking for everyone. Maurice had lost his beloved wife, Will lost his beautiful mum, whilst Eloise had lost her best friend, a second mum to her, yet here she was, about to meet this precious woman who had always meant the world to her. From the very first time she had met her, she was welcomed into her home with open arms, and she was made to feel part of the family from day one. Mary Devoir had a beautiful heart, and Eloise was always grateful to her for all the love and support she gave her and always thankful to her for offering guidance when she needed it. She always made herself available to listen, like a mother with her daughter. As butterflies drifted through the air, Eloise was grateful for the peace of the morning that was soul soothing, being such a delight with every step she took, admiring all the amazing views around her with its picturesque landscapes of beauty. As the morning developed, the sounds of young birds began to fill the air with their chirps. 'Oh look!' She cried as scurrying squirrels ran in front of them, searching for food under leafy canopies of the woodland. 'You will find a lot of them here,' he smiled, as the enchanting views that surrounded them grew increasingly captivating just as they proceeded ahead, and Eloise was still enthralled at every inch of beauty that appeared before her.

A middle-aged woman sat sewing beneath a cherry blossom tree, as pink petals wafted around her in the gentle breeze, and Eloise recognised her immediately as Mary Devoir. Her silver-grey hair framed her perfectly round face, whilst the heavenly light added a golden tint to her cheeks as she sat in this glorious place. 'Mum,' Will whispered, so as not to startle her, as Mary glanced up from her embroidery that lay neatly in her lap. Her angelic smile lit up her face when she saw Eloise standing there before her. 'Eloise,' she cried. 'My dear, dear daughter!' She had often called Eloise her daughter as they had always been so close, and having just the one son, she felt blessed for having that mother-daughter bond. Eloise shed a tear as she stepped forward, and Mary stooped to greet her as she hugged her tight. 'You look so well,' Eloise remarked. 'Thank you,' she replied, hugging her tight. 'It must be the pure air that we breathe here,' she declared, with a smile on her face at the joy of seeing Eloise after such a long time. 'Although there is no oxygen in heaven,' Will vowed. 'The air that we breathe here is the presence of God, and every breath you take refreshes you.' Eloise smiled, grateful for all that she was beginning to learn in this heavenly land. 'Would you care for a cold drink?' Mary questioned as she proceeded to lead the way into her home. 'Oh, that would be lovely.' She and Will followed her into her spacious abode, which had been exactly as Eloise imagined Mary Devoir's home to be. Filled with the exact furniture that Mary adored and displayed with as many ornaments and knick-knacks as she had in her previous life. 'As you can see,' Will commented. 'Mother still likes to have all her ornaments around her.' For a second, Eloise could not help but have a little giggle to herself. 'Mmmmmmm. I know someone else who would happily have a house full of ornaments if he had his way.' She gazed a smile in Will's direction, his face looking a little flushed. The room had a vast amount of space, with the sofas being exactly as Eloise had imagined. Elegant with their scrolled armrests and their triple raised, castor foot legs, oozing luxury and glamour, whilst an extensive range of ornaments filled every nook and cranny in this magnificent room that made it Mary's home, just the way she liked it. 'Why don't you go and sit down, while I get you your drink?' Mary suggested. The chat flowed continuously, and Eloise was grateful for the ice-cold drink that she sipped from in between their conversation. Mary's speech was slow, still having to take a minute or two to think about what she wanted to say before talking, but Eloise was not shocked at all at how she could still hold a conversation for a great length of time. 'Let me show you something,' Mary beamed, as she slowly walked across to the other side of the room where a beautiful basket sat, wrapped in its stunning, bold, patterned fabric. Opening the lid, she gently lifted out the most exquisite blankets that Eloise had ever seen. 'These are the cross-stitch covers I have been working on,' she explained. 'I have been making them for the babies here.' Eloise was astounded by the vibrant colours and elaborate details that Mary had put into these most stunning pieces of work. 'Oh my, how absolutely beautiful are these,' she praised Mary, overwhelmed by the hard work that she had put into each blanket with its intricate accents and unique style. They were perfect for the little ones. 'Oh Mary, they are unquestionably the most decorative and outstanding pieces of needlework I have ever seen,' Eloise leant over and hugged her as she complimented her once again. 'What a beautiful thing to be doing for all these sweet babies,' she cried. 'Oh, we all help where we can,' Mary replied, as she made a small gesture to Eloise.

'There are many things you can help out with, my dear,' she assured. 'Oh, I would be truly honoured to help wherever I am able to,' Eloise confirmed with a smile. As they talked away, recalling many memories that they had made on earth and all the new memories they had to look forward to here in heaven together, neither was aware of the time, for there was no measurement of 'time' here; they were more like 'Periods.' Periods of pleasure and praising of joy and peace, and Eloise was grateful for every moment she had spent here so far and all that she had to look forward to in this beautiful land that was now her home. 'Where is father?' Asked Will, expecting him to be about. 'Oh,' answered Mary. 'You know your father, he will be about, on one of his walks, no doubt chatting to someone somewhere,' she went on. Maurice passed away just a few weeks after Will. Everyone had reckoned that he could not take any more, which was not surprising after losing his wife, then his son. Eloise was so upset when he died, and even struggled at his funeral, as she had always been grateful to him for taking good care of her after Will passed away. It was like losing another member of the family, but here she was now in this beautiful place with them all once again.

After some time spent with Mary, Will suggested that she should get some rest and that he and Eloise would come to see her again. 'My dearest daughter,' Mary said as she hugged Eloise tightly. 'It has been so lovely to see you and spend this wonderful moment with you. I will see you again.' 'Yes, you will.' Eloise answered, nodding her head. 'Most definitely.' Will leaned forward as his mother embraced him. 'There,' she said, patting his back. 'Now you be getting on your way and show Eloise some more of this beautiful land.' 'Yes, mother, I shall, and there will be no doubt that we shall see you again soon,' answered Will, as he placed a gentle kiss upon the side of his mother's cheek.

After leaving Mary's home and just a short distance away, Eloise spotted, in amongst a group of children, a man speaking and touching the word of God, and knew in her mind that it must have been Paul the Apostle.

Here he stood, so authentic, so loving as he spread the teachings of Jesus to these beautiful children, as they sat huddled up together, listening to every word that was being taught to them. She noticed, as each child spoke, that he took a moment to listen to what each of them had to say, answering any questions that they had asked, with gentleness and kindness. Eloise stood for a moment, intrigued at these little ones, as they sat looking and taking in every word that was being spoken to them, whilst they listened to the gentleness of the Apostle's calming voice. 'Oh, how wonderful heaven is,' she cried out. 'There is so much to see here,' she said, as she slowly walked ahead with Will. 'There are so many paths and trails leading to such beautiful places that I would never have dreamt even existed.' 'Oh, there really are,' answered

Will as he took Eloise's hand in his and continued to lead the way. 'There is so much more for you to see, my love, and so many more people for you to meet.' Excitedly, Eloise followed on in Will's footsteps. 'But, in time,' he stated. 'We will have a short break before we go on.' Eloise nodded with a smile, appreciative of all that Will was showing her. They sat down on a bench that was beside what Eloise believed to be an allotment of some sort, as beautiful purple flowers trailed across the trellising of the small plot. It was one of the many things that Eloise had noticed in this captivating place, that apart from the stunning scenery, the surroundings were picturesque and extremely well looked after. Whilst resting, several small birds swiftly flew by, and as they caught Eloise's eye, she immediately recognised the elderly man who was slouched in a chair just a few feet away from her. She walked towards the fence that encircled the plot and observed the man sitting in the wooden rocking chair. She could not help but have a little giggle to herself at the way in which the handkerchief sat resting on his head. His eyes were closed whilst his short grey hair blew gently in the breeze as Eloise leant towards the fence, 'Grandad!' She called, in her gentlest of voices, but the man did not stir, just sat, sleeping. He always loved to relax and take it easy.

Hendrix passed away several years after Bea, Eloise's nan, and it was always surprising that he had managed to carry on for as long as he did after losing his beloved wife. He was a loving and affectionate man with a huge heart and the kindest of eyes, always full of so much love and generosity.

Leaving her grandad to continue with his nap, both Eloise and Will set out on their way. The day dawned crisp and clear as they walked in and out amongst the trees, and just as Eloise was enjoying the pure serenity that filled her, a repetitive laughing was suddenly heard close by, startling her. 'What was that?' She asked nervously, unfamiliar with the sudden loud noise. 'That was a kookaburra.' Will added. Two of them were spotted in the large tree to the side of him, their white heads and underparts, along with their dark brown wings, could be seen quite evidently, as their brown eyed stripes peered through the branches. 'Known for staying in their close-knit family groups,' Will added, as he picked some fruit and handed it to Eloise. 'Take this.' 'What is it?' She questioned with a puzzled look upon her face. 'It is a Monstera Deliciosa fruit, they will eat that out of your hand,' Will confirmed. 'I have never seen anything like this before,' she remarked, looking at the long ear of corn, covered in green scales. 'It is a combination of pineapple, guava and mango,' commented Will. 'They love it.' As Eloise held out two pieces of fruit, one by one, the kookaburras gently took them from her hand. 'Oh my!' She cried. 'I cannot believe how gentle they are. 'They will let you rub their bellies, too,' Will chuckled, and with that, Eloise gently stroked them on their front.

As they continued their walk through forests, past big old oak trees with their wide trunks and crumpled leaves, and branches swaying, there was something exhilarating about being in this heavenly place, Eloise thought, with its beautiful sights and sounds. A God's blessing of true beauty, a place where everything stood still and where it brought a total sense of peace.

CHAPTER 9

Once back, Eloise rested for what felt like a long period, although not aware of how long she had been asleep for, but woke to the sound of gospel singers, as a beautiful harmony of enthusiasm and passion filled the air. Gentle sounds of birds chirped outside the window, and golden fingers of light poured through, lighting up the room, as Will cupped her chin in his hand and kissed her soft, tender lips. She stretched her limbs, letting out a contented sigh, as she accepted his hand and made her way outside into the glorious setting that stood before her, taking in a deep breath as she inhaled the fresh, crisp air that embraced the beauty of all that surrounded her.

Dew on the blades of grass sparkled in the sunlight as they strolled along a pathway, a golden path that led directly to a lake. Eloise stopped in her tracks and gazed wondrously towards the edge of it, as it greeted her with warmth, beauty, and serenity. It was at that moment, she spotted a man sat on an oak wood chair, a notebook at his side and a pen tucked neatly behind his ear, with his nose in a book. His pure white gown hung to his ankles as his bare feet peeked out below, and as Eloise drew closer, it was only then that she recognised the man. 'Eli?' She hesitated for a moment, until the man glanced up and only then did she realise it was him. Her wonderful, caring, thoughtful stepdad, looking the same handsome, suave man that she remembered, with his short, dark hair, glasses and even in his simple robe, he was still well presented. 'Eloise?' 'Yes,' she cried. 'It is me.' It was at that moment that he wrapped his arms around his stepdaughter as they hugged each other tightly. 'Oh, how good it does feel to see you again,' Eloise cried, as she stepped back and took a good look at this suave man who stood before her. 'It has been so long,' Eli answered, as he held her tightly against his chest, then as he nudged her gently away, 'Let me look at you. Still as beautiful as always.' Eloise smiled bashfully. 'Bless you.' 'Hello again, Eli. I see you are at your usual place,' Will smiled. 'Oh yes, you know me all too well,' he replied with a firm grip of Will's hand, giving it a good shake, just as he had always done.

'How beautiful is the water, what a wonderful sight,' Eloise said to Will and Eli as she stepped forward. 'Are all the lakes like this one?' 'Similar,' Will replied, as he looked at Eloise with tenderness in his eyes. 'This is angelic,' she whispered, as the lake, with its calmness, rippled softly around her. Eli loved the lake, this one especially, as it was joined by a pine forest, and he enjoyed the peace and quiet and tranquillity in this haven. It was all too often that he would be sat alone, and it was just how he liked it, taking in all the glory that surrounded him. 'I am going to give you and Eli some space,' said Will with a warm smile. 'You both have a lot to catch up on.' 'I can walk her back later,' Eli offered 'It is not a problem.' 'I guess I will see you back at the house then?' Eloise closed in, giving Will a warm hug, then, after kissing her cheek gently, he walked off in the opposite direction.

Eli was one of the gentlest men and had the most caring nature. He stood out for the kindness and advice he gave others, including Eloise, which always helped her throughout her life. He always abided by morals, such as respect for people, honesty, and discipline, but he always protected and provided for Eloise, and she treasured all the memories that she had made with him in all the years she had known him.

Making her way through the sights, sounds and smells of the pine forest, the trees danced in the breeze as their branches swayed two and thro, each one standing tall and proud, their leaves ablaze in gorgeous shades of orange, yellows, reds, and browns, creating a stunning display. She was led into a completely different direction, on a path she had not been down before, feeling so happy, whilst talking nonstop, admiring the beauty of the forest that continued to surround her. It was pure and clean, as though it had never been disturbed by walkers before, as a breeze bustled through the branches of the pine trees, making the leaves flutter like confetti, the whole forest swaying, creating a soothing sound that was pure heaven to anyone's ears. It was breathtaking, as the light filtered through them, scattering patches onto the forest floor as each twig creaked beneath her feet, and as she shuffled through, birds could be heard singing sweetly as they flew from branch to branch. The air was crisp and fresh in this captivating world, a place of solace, a place of serenity and harmony, and Eloise began to feel increasingly carefree, mesmerised by the continuous peace as she lifted her face, letting the warmth dance across her skin. It was just a few steps more before she came to a long gravel path that extended from one end of the forest to the other, the stones being that of a mixture of colours, colours from the rainbow to be precise, her favourite was the pink, as it stood out the brightest and sparkled like a diamond. At the end of the path, a plot with an assortment of homes stood widespread, some were more of a cabin look than a house, so Eloise thought! 'Mine is just up here on the right,' Eli pointed out what looked like a huge palace! 'This is Moonlight Meadow.' 'My word!' Cried Eloise. 'This is stunning.' She took in the beauty that surrounded the house with every colour of Lily you could possibly ever imagine, from bright yellow to deep orange, not forgetting the delicate white ones. Beautiful and elegant as they stood proud around the entrance of the house. 'You know the lilies here in heaven symbolise love, faith and hope,' vowed Eli, with a smile. 'Flowers also serve as reminders of God's presence and love,' he confirmed. 'How amazing is this?' Eloise cried. 'And to have the pine forest at the back of your house! This is simply beautiful,' she uttered, still trying to take in the exquisite array of flowers that stood before her. 'Come, let me show you inside.' Eli took her by the hand as they entered the welcoming home, greeted by a spacious entrance, and as an openness of light shone right through, Eloise could not quite get over how beautiful such an entrance could be! The white walls filled the large space with a sense of cleanliness and freshness, and an airiness of lightness and delicacy, whilst the hallway sat adjacent to a wide staircase with its fifteen-foot ceiling, which she assumed led to several bedrooms; however, she did not look at those, but instead, paid attention to what was on the ground floor. Moving further along, Eli guided her into the kitchen, where she was once again taken aback by the beauty of it, as a fair number of units filled the space, standing proud with their grey marble worktops and white cupboard doors, and every appliance you could possibly need. The house was complete with its large arched windows that let in every bit of light possible, illuminating the whiteness of every tiled floor, with its marble flowing effortlessly into every single room. 'Simply heavenly,' Eloise cried, as her eyes drifted from the amazing scenery, and as they took in all that surrounded her, she suddenly got a feeling of calmness and serenity within herself. She entered the lounge through a large archway that stood beyond her and was immediately drawn to the tantalising mixture of aromas coming from the sweet-scented potpourri, its aromatic dried flowers and lemon slice were releasing a refreshing and uplifting fragrance, creating a welcome that Eloise was very grateful for. The glamorous room was where grandeur meets stylish in its magnificent setting that drew her in, with its mirrored walls giving a sophisticated touch to the room, whilst the soft lighting and expensive fabric created the exquisite look that finished the large space to all its glory. The décor of the room was tastefully elegant, with its cream cotton curtains hanging in their luxurious design. 'I love this,' said Eloise. 'Every detail here is of love and style, such taste.' 'Thank you, I have tried to create a masterpiece in every corner of the house,' answered Eli as he pushed open the double glass doors that led out onto the beautiful garden. A sense of tranquillity washed over Eloise, along with a scent of freshness coming from the cut grass that lay like a blanket of dew, as it glistened like a bed of diamonds in the pure light of day. She was once again astounded by the assortment of colours and beauty all around her as shrubs of all colours filled every space of the immaculate garden, whilst roses, petunias, lilacs, and chrysanthemums stood displayed, as they filled the air with their pleasant, sweet smells.

Eloise sat beside her stepfather on the cushioned step at the bottom of the garden. It was a peaceful spot, Elis' favourite spot, where he quite often sat and read or sketched a few drawings. They talked about his final moment before he passed away. 'I remember it well, and still recall you and your mum, sitting at my bedside,' he whispered. 'Yes,' uttered Eloise. 'We sat for a long time, just looking at you, and waiting, hoping so much that you would open your eyes, but that wasn't to be,' she added. 'We had only popped home for a short while, and the second we got in the door, the phone rang, and it was the hospital to say you had passed away.' 'I didn't want you and your mum to see me go,' Eli continued. 'I knew there was no way back to what had happened to me, so I went peacefully, and the next thing I knew, I was here in heaven.' 'It was horrible that I wasn't able to say a proper goodbye to you,' Eloise replied, with sadness in her voice. Eli leant forward and gave his stepdaughter a comforting hug, just as a rustling in one of the shrubs startled her. 'Hey, little one, are you coming to say hello?' She tried to coax the little robin out from the bush, but it was having none of it.

Instead, it poked its head out the once, then flew away.

It seemed like quite a while was spent at her stepfather's home chatting, and now, she was on her way to see something else he had longed to show her. Eli led the way out of the house, and they walked side by side as birds' sweet tones sang into a glorious chorus. 'You know something,' said Eloise, as she set forth in the direction in which Eli was taking her. 'I never told you before that you were such an important person in my life. I never told you how much I always loved you,' she continued. 'Or how much I appreciated all that you did for me.' Eli stopped in his tracks and faced Eloise with a smile. 'I knew. I always knew.' He went on. 'You never had to tell me, because you showed it in everything you did. You, my love,' he said, 'You quite simply have the kindest and warmest of hearts.' Eloise felt quite emotional as she hugged her stepfather gently. 'Don't let anyone ever tell you any different,' he added, as he gave a gentle squeeze in return.

A light breeze blew a gentle scent of sweet, yet pungent smell of pine throughout the air, and as Eloise turned the corner, she stood wide-eyed in amazement at the beautiful building in front of her, as rays of light touched down onto the modern building, each coloured piece of glass illuminated like a dazzling city. Its towering pillars gave a sense of awe, and she was astounded by the beauty, which brought a smile to her face as she looked around, taking in every single detail. 'What a magnificent vision,' she put forward, gazing at its huge, solid oak door. Engraved with the face of God, it shimmered towards her as it glowed in the golden light. As Eli slowly turned the knob, it creaked open, exposing a musky smell, a woody, earthy smell, Eloise thought, although barely taking any notice of that as she was more captivated by the thousands of files and scrolls that were stacked high to the ceiling. Never had she seen anything like it! 'Wow!' She cried out, turning to her stepfather with a look of wonder. 'Piles of information must be in here?' 'Shelves and shelves of information of every single person that has arrived in heaven stands proudly on every shelf,' Eli explained. 'This is the Records Room. All the records of people's past, and failures, every good and bad thing they have done, everything from the beginning of time is recorded and kept safely,' he went on. 'Every tear that has been shed has been recorded.' Greatly impressed, but feeling rather emotional, Eloise wiped a tear away from her watery eye, for she could not believe that she was standing in yet another exquisite building in this beautiful land. The whole area of space was as peaceful as a nature reserve and a magical place, where you could get totally lost in. 'We are not really supposed to come in here,' Eli spoke softly. 'Then we must leave quickly and quietly,' Eloise answered in a sharpish manner. 'Can we go back to the lake?' 'I will take you to another one where Will shall be waiting for you.' He pulled the heavy door shut, locked it behind him, and led the way to the lake, and sure enough, Will was stood waiting just before it. He glanced at Eloise with a smile as swans glided along the edge of the bank and a gaggle of geese grazed almost beside them. 'We shall see one another real soon, and thank you for walking me back,' said Eloise, and with a warm embrace, Eli hugged her. 'You are more than welcome. I look forward to seeing you again soon.' 'Most definitely,' assured Eloise as she kissed her stepfather farewell and watched him walk in the opposite direction.

CHAPTER 10

'Did you have a remarkable catch-up with Eli?' Will asked his beloved with a warm smile. 'Oh, it was so lovely to see him again,' Eloise answered, as she placed her hand in his. 'Come, my precious one. Let me show you something, something so beautiful.' Eloise was intrigued as she followed in his footsteps along a wooded path, sauntering along, taking in every beautiful piece of paradise along the way, as it enveloped her in this world of timeless beauty. In the distance, she could hear rushing water and in a blink of an eye, discovered something so picturesque, like nothing she had ever seen before. 'Goodness!' Was all she could voice, absolutely awestruck by what she could only ever imagine to be in a dream, yet here she stood in this beautiful place. 'Charmingly breathtaking,' she commented. 'Isn't it just,' he replied, returning her smile. Eloise just stood for a moment as she took in all the exquisiteness that lay in front of her and around her in this glorious place, which she now called home. At the foot of the slope, where she stood, the ground was sprinkled with an assortment of colours, an array of stunning flowers. 'How on earth can this all be possible!' She gasped to herself, admiring the magnificent beauty that lay in front of her eyes, and like a wall of blue satin, a waterfall tumbled down a mountain, being the most spectacular waterfall she had ever seen, surging and plunging down into the most gorgeous lake below. You could see through it as if it were a piece of glass, and like a huge waterspout, it foamed its way to the bottom, into the most blissful, blue lake you ever did see. The sight was spectacular, and as Eloise drew even closer to it, she half expected the sound to get louder from the gushing of the water dropping into the lake below, but instead, it was the calmest and quietest of waterfalls she had ever heard, and as the splendid beauty touched her gently, she embraced it with appreciation.

The heavenly light added a golden tint to the face of the lake, and it was paradise, as frogs leapt out of the water, their slender bodies and long legs slapping the surface as they sank back amongst the purple lilies that glided across the top. The light breeze felt good as it brushed against Eloise's cheek as she stood taking in the flawlessness of her life here in this graceful beauty. 'It is absolutely exquisite,' she said. 'I bet you have written many a chapter here.' Will glanced in her direction with a smile. 'Yes, I have,' he beamed. 'But sometimes I just come and sit down by the water and take in all the glorious light and the quietness all around. It is so peaceful.' Will had always been a keen writer, just like Eloise, and in his lifetime had written many books. She had always wondered how he would have coped without his writing after he had passed away, yet here he was, with the most peacefulness you could ever possibly want. What better place to write a book!

The scenery was as striking as paradise, and the grass beneath her was a cushion of green, like a soft heaven-weaved quilt, and as each blade shimmered in the light and moved in the breeze, Eloise could not help but soak in the colours of all the stunning flowers that filled the place with a sweet fragrance. It was impossible to feel anything but tranquillity in a place that covered itself in such beauty. Stopping for a moment, she took in the glorious sight that lay in front of her, which enhanced the quiet and peaceful beauty of the scene. No sound sang out from the shimmering emptiness of space around her as she sat down beside Will, admiring the glorious lustre of the water, feeling totally relaxed. Several thoughts entered her head as she closed her eyes, recalling all the amazing things she had seen so far, feeling so at peace with all that surrounded her. She was not entirely sure of how long it had been since she had slipped into a little world of her own, but was startled by Will peering over her with a warm smile, and as she sat up, he took her hand in his and kissed the back of it gently. 'Come,' he whispered. 'I have somewhere else I must take you.' Eloise was intrigued and rose to her feet sharpish as Will led the way.

Many paths led to so many captivating places, she thought, as she followed in his footsteps, taking in the glorious warmth that covered the surrounding area with a golden tranquillity. Amongst the narrow paths that lie ahead, were clusters of bright yellow sundrops, each one attracting beautiful butterflies whose wings were in a variety of colours as they flew in the gentle breeze above. Each path led to somewhere different, and it was always exciting to see where each one came out. Eloise noticed that each of them was unlike any path she had ever seen, for they were of pure gold, with an array of white pebbles on either side that shone like a beam of light, directing the way. Each part of heaven she had been shown was increasingly beautiful, and Eloise could not believe such a place could be so full of wonder. Just a few more steps and there in front of her was the most picturesque of pictures. She had never seen such beauty as that of where she was right now, and with every step she took, there was another mass of warmth and serenity. 'How magnificent,' she cried out, as she drew closer to the spectacular sight that lay before her eyes. A gem blue stream stood before her in what felt like a hidden forest, as pebbles whisked about under the water like pieces of glitter and chords of light sparkled down from above, bathing its surface in gold. 'It is pure, refreshing water. You can drink it if you wish to,' Will stated. As Eloise slowly dipped her hand under the cold water, she collected a few drops and slid them into her mouth and much to her surprise, it was fresh water.

The lake was surprisingly empty, all bar a few children and adults, and Eloise could not help but smile at the joy on the children's faces as she stood and gazed out at the sheer wonder that was in front of her, as it was the first time she had ever seen such beauty in a lake. She stood and watched as the warm rays touched the surface, whilst the green lawn, gentle on the soles of her feet, provided her with a softness between her toes. Glancing towards Will with a smile, she laid down beside him, sinking into the soft grass and closed her sauntering eyes as she breathed in the fresh scent that was in the air, letting out a lengthy sigh of sheer relaxation and delight, and no sooner had she shut them, they were open again, as a warm sensation fell upon her face. Sitting up, she looked across the lake and caught sight of a slightly podgy woman, stooped over washing her hands in the clear water, and she immediately recognised Alicia, her grandma, her father's mum. She would distinguish her face and mass of wavy, white hair anywhere. As she walked up to her, Alicia turned to face her Granddaughter, her sparkling blue eyes smiling. 'Eloise, my dear, how wonderful to see you here.' Eloise hugged her grandma gently and could not help but notice that her hands, which were once very much calloused from years of washing and gardening, were now the softest and gentlest. 'Are you okay, Grandma?' She questioned. 'Yes, dear, I feel wonderful, the air here is so pure, and it is so peaceful,' Alicia answered. 'Oh, hello Will, so good to see you again, too, dear.' Will leaned forward and gave Alicia a warm hug. 'You too,' he responded with a smile. Alicia had always been a strong woman and very hardworking. She was never one to be afraid to say how it was and, more often than not, was outspoken, but people always admired her for that. Underneath all that, though, she was quite gentle and had a lot of respect and understanding for whoever she spoke to. 'Where is grandpa?' Eloise asked. 'Oh, he is back at the cottage, you know, your grandpa, he was never one for doing much, he always preferred to just sit around.' Eloise giggled, knowing her gran was completely right.

Albie was always a hardworking man back in his day, but as he became older, he liked the easy things in life, and if that meant doing less, then he was sure to lap that up. Eloise did not really know much about her grandpa, Albie, as she was very young when he passed away; however, she did always remember that he was a very tall man and that Jax took after him in that way. 'I can take you to see him if you like in a short while, and show you around the cottage too,' promised Alicia. 'That would be wonderful, Grandma, thank you.' Eloise's gaze returned to the gracefulness of the lake in front of her, and with every breath she took, a smell of purity lifted her, making her feel freer than she had ever felt. 'This is such a stunning lake,' beamed Eloise. 'The setting is full of such calmness and beauty.' 'Have you seen the River of Paradise yet, my dear?' Alicia questioned. 'No, Grandma, where is that at?' 'Come, Will and I shall take you there.' They took a leisurely walk as Eloise did not want to hurry her grandma in case she was to find it a little difficult, but the more they walked, the more she could not help but notice the bounce she had in her step. 'Are you okay?' She questioned, surprised at the speed she was going. 'Yes, my dear,' assured Alicia. 'Why do you ask? 'Oh!' Eloise hesitated for a second. 'No reason.' She assured her grandma as they proceeded ahead.

A cool breeze flooded through the magnificent trees as they continued their walk through the grasses of pure green. Everywhere was so exquisite that Eloise wanted to observe and take in all that surrounded her, in this magical place that gave her a warm sensation throughout her body. The view of what she could see ahead whispered softly to her as she drew closer. 'This is the River of Paradise,' Alicia declared with a smile, as they now stood in front of what Eloise believed to be something quite stunning, that she was simply lost for words, and was more captivated than her mind could ever imagine. 'The rivers flow from the garden of Eden and splits into four,' added Alicia. 'Each one flowing in a different direction,' piped up Will. 'They each have a purpose, and each of those purposes symbolises life. Basically,' said Will. 'As it flows out of Eden, it waters the garden and from there it divides and becomes four rivers.' 'Oh,' cried out Eloise passionately as she questioned the comment, not really understanding what was meant. 'And?' 'Let me explain,' added Will, and in deep thought, carried on the conversation. 'Each of the rivers has a meaning, one of the meanings is full flowing, which kind of makes sense, because God wants us all to experience the full flow of his presence.' 'Oh, I love that,' Eloise added. 'The second, meaning gushing or

bursting forth, which again has a special meaning.'
'Which is?' Eloise asked, waiting patiently for an
answer. 'God is focusing on what everyone here in
heaven can contribute to others. More so than what
we need or want for ourselves,' he added. 'The third
river,' piped up Alicia, 'means swift, to be quick, to
have an aim, to have a goal in sight, and to move
towards fulfilling those goals, with God's help, of
course, and finally, the fourth river,' she went on.
'Means sweet and fruitful. But it is not just for our
benefit either,' she added, raising her brows and
smiling. 'It means to spread knowledge to one another
here in heaven, of God, and that way, you will
continue to be blessed as the rivers flow.' 'What
beautiful messages each of these rivers represent,'
added Eloise, feeling quite emotional. 'And did you
know?' Will added. 'The word river,' is named
'Nahar, which means to shine, light, and beam. To be
radiant, to flow.' 'That is quite charming,' voiced
Eloise as she smiled at both Will and her grandma.'
She could not believe how much she was learning
since she had come to this beautiful land, and she
believed that all the information she was acquiring
was likely to bring her closer to God.

CHAPTER 11

Towering trees surrounded Eloise as she carried on
with the walk through the woods, taking in every
scent that filled her nose from the array of flowers that
stood before her, and as the leaves from the branches
brushed up against her hair and a gentle breeze tickled
her face, it was at that moment that she chose to rest at
the side of a large conifer tree, as both Will and her
grandma joined her, whilst sparrows fluttered above
their heads. She vastly appreciated all that she was
being taught in heaven, but knowing also that there
was so much more to learn in this exquisite place.
'Heaven is such a paradise,' she stated, as she looked
all around where she was sitting at that precise
moment, taking in all the beauty, whilst recalling all
the wonder that she had seen so far. 'Oh yes, my
dear,' replied Alicia, 'and there is so much to learn
here, but I believe that we must let those who come
here find their own path, with a little help from one
another, of course,' she added, with a smile. Eloise
smiled back at her grandmother as flowers of vibrant
hues caught her eye as they blew gently, and she was
mesmerised by the beautiful array of colour that
surrounded her, appreciating every single one.
Daisies, marigolds, amongst others, created a
harmonious balance as Eloise inhaled the sweet scents
that filled the air. After spending a little time with her
thoughts, taking in all that she had seen and trying to

understand every word that had been said to her, Grandma Alicia had decided on making her way back to her home. 'Come on, Eloise,' she announced. 'I will take you to my cottage, show you around, and we will wake Grandpa up.' Eloise chuckled as Will said his goodbyes to both her and Alicia, hugging them both as he bid farewell for the time being.

A tune of voices of perfect pitch could be heard in the distance as they sauntered back along the woodland path, as beams of light peeked through the canopied trees. As they strolled along past streets of gold, walls of precious stone were illuminated by the glory of God, and Eloise came to feel totally at home in beautiful heaven, with not just the family members she had met up with, but the gracefulness of the place and all that she had seen so far. A gravel track which ran down the middle of the main golden path sat just ahead, and it made Eloise realise just how beautiful heaven really was as she observed and took in all that it had to offer. Bordered by pink and purple flowers, whilst a mixture of Lobelia and Primroses (also known as pink ladies) bloomed in the open air. Several grown-ups and children passed them by, every one of them said a hello with a smile, all were so kind, so Eloise thought.

A small cottage sat just a little distance away, surrounded by a cluster of trees, with every fruit imaginable, from apples, pears, peaches, to plums, blueberries, and kiwis. 'Here we are.' Alicia stopped at the quaintest of cottages and, nudging the iron gate open, she led the way through. 'This is Bluebell Cottage.' The garden was small but compact with many pots, filled with hundreds and hundreds of Bluebells, all you could imagine, and Eloise was drawn in by the scent of every one that stood before her. She had never seen so many blooming in one place, and it took her breath away. Making her way up the shingled path, Eloise was aware that it was a typical porch of an elderly couple, well, that of her Grandma Alicia and Grandpa Albie anyway. The front door was a little creaky as her grandmother nudged it open and led the way into the cottage itself, as a smell of fresh bread wafted up throughout, that of a typical day of baking, so Eloise thought, as she entered the cottage, and noticed it had a certain charm about it, which made it feel like a special home. 'Come in, come in, my dear,' Alicia directed her Granddaughter through the narrow hallway, which was filled with hundreds of photographs lining every inch of wall space. The carpet, a mottled green, ran from the entrance all the way through into the small lounge, which again was filled with every ornament and knick-knack you could possibly ever need! Eloise looked around the room at what felt like Aladdin's cave, every corner taken up with every piece of furniture possible, cramped into every little bit of space, leaving no room to move. Although not overly spacious, it was just the right size for her Grandparents.

Whilst Alicia had gone to wake Gramps up, Eloise took herself out into the garden. It was small, but filled with rows and rows of flowers, all different varieties and colours, arranged and formed in symmetrical lines. The lawn lay like a freshly laid carpet, as white slabs sat from the start of the garden to the very end, making a pathway that led to a small wooden table, where two chairs were tucked neatly on either side of it, and fitted with soft cushioned seating. Eloise could not help but smile as the house and garden reminded her so much of what she could remember seeing when she was a child and visited her grandparents every Saturday. Holding that thought, she entered the rear door and made her way back towards the living room, but not before going into the kitchen and taking in the sweet smell of the bread that had been baking. The room was small, but it had a warmth to it, and the countertops, although cluttered with pots and plates, still had a certain charm and character. A vintage/retro larder cupboard stood up against the main wall, and again, Eloise smiled, remembering the exact one that her grandparents had in their home when she was little. A free-standing cabinet with a drop-down leaf worktop, which served as a workspace, but also featured a top glass door cabinet for storage and a cupboard underneath, fitted with a shelf. Eloise suddenly recalled all the times she used to help her grandma to make sandwiches at the workstation she had herself! 'Your grandpa is just coming now,' Alicia called out as she entered the kitchen. 'Please, go and take a seat, my dear.' Eloise tried to find a space on the sofa, clearing a few books that sat piled up. She wondered how her grandma and grandpa lived in amongst so much stuff, but she also understood that it was all their memories, and that was what mattered. Alicia trundled on through to the lounge, with a small glass of lemon juice and a slice of freshly baked bread, still warm as the knob of butter melted immediately. 'Here you go, my dear.' She handed both the juice and the bread over. 'Thank you,' Eloise replied. It was not long after that her grandpa entered the room.

Albie was a tall man of about six feet and not a lot of hair. Thinking about it now, he reminded Eloise of the BFG, with his long, pointed face, projecting nose and large ears. He had to duck the doorway as he walked into the living room, and as Eloise stood and looked up at him, his once aged eyes and time-worn skin gleamed, along with his amiable smile. She always remembered he was tall, but not that tall! She felt quite tiny, standing beside him. 'Look at you all grown up. The last time I saw you, you were a wee thing.' He hugged Eloise gently. 'Sit down, young one,' he mumbled, pointing to the sofa. 'Finish your bread. Your Grandma's hands worked hard making that.' 'Eloise.' Alicia spoke out. 'Have you seen your dad yet?' 'No, not yet, but soon though, I hope. It has been so long. I have missed him so much.' 'It must have been such a shock for you when he passed,' spoke Albie. 'Yes, it really was. But now I am here, I shall make sure I make up for lost time.' 'And you will, my dear,' Alicia answered. 'You get to be with us all.'

Eloise chatted with her Grandparents a while longer, about some of the things that she could remember, although sadly, Grandpa Albie was not around then, as he had already passed away. She could only recall the times she had visited her grandmother, where countless family moments were had every Saturday, with her parents, when they used to sit and watch the wrestling. 'Do you remember Grandma? You used to shout out Kick him in the -----.' 'Yes, I remember,' Alicia laughed as she smiled at her Granddaughter. She always took her wrestling seriously, and Eloise and her sisters always found it quite funny, although Dad was never impressed and always gave that swift glance towards his mother. 'I also remember how all the furniture in the living room had to be pushed back so the table could be opened in the middle of the room at teatime.' 'Yes, that sounds like your grandma,' chipped in Albie. 'And us kids had to lay the table with the necessary cutlery, and we always had scrambled eggs on toast,' chuckled Eloise. 'Oh!' She added. What about when you used to call out the football pools results, and we had to be silent, or we would get that look off you, Grandma.' Alicia always had that stare, and the kids knew then to keep quiet. 'You have a very good memory,' piped up Albie. 'They were such good times.' Eloise looked up at her grandpa with a smile. They may have only been small things to anyone else, but to Eloise, they were a lifetime of happy memories and being where she was now held so much warmth and love, and she felt so happy, knowing she had more of these moments to spend with her Grandparents and being able to make new memories too.

After what seemed like a long time of reminiscing with them, she bid farewell for the time being and made her way back to her own home. Dropping onto the padded sofa and resting her head on one of the arms, she positioned herself within this haven that soothed her soul as she closed her eyes and thought about all that had happened that day. It was not long before she had dozed off, happy at all she had seen so far and looking forward to all that was still ahead of her.

CHAPTER 12

After a short rest, Eloise woke feeling fresh, as the light poured through the window, bringing new hopes for the remainder of the day. 'Hello beautiful,' said Will, as he leant in and gave her a gentle kiss. Eloise was not aware that she had dozed off and so was a little startled, but returned the kiss with affection. 'I am so in love with you,' she told him. His smile was tender as he leaned towards her, 'I am so in love with you too,' he replied as he kissed her again. 'Come, my love, I would like to take you somewhere.' She smiled gratefully as Will helped her to her feet, unaware of where she was going to be going this time, but was happy at wherever he was to take her, whether it be meeting members of the family, or looking at the stunning places that surrounded her. She stretched as she got up off the couch, as excitement ran through her, enthusiastic to get outside. 'Where are we going?' She asked as she proceeded to follow Will. 'I am going to show you the beach.' 'A beach?' Questioned Eloise. 'Is there really a beach here?' 'There is for certain, come, let me take you to it, it is magnificent.'

Eloise felt a peaceful feeling overwhelm her as she waded through the stunning canopy of the woodland, as trees towered over her and branches twisted in and out amongst one another. The walk was pure serenity, where a carpet of leaves lined the pathway as she followed the scurrying squirrels that searched for something to eat. Eloise was overwhelmed by the number of different directions there were to take in this beautiful place, so much to see, she thought, quickening her step, eager to see more, knowing she was getting closer, as she could smell the salt air and hear the faint sound of the waves. 'Just through here,' Will pointed at a large archway just in front of them. But this was not some wooden arch with lattice side panels and spikes holding it into the ground. No! This was an extraordinary archway made of gold. Beautiful and stylish, Eloise thought as she admired the huge piece that stood before her. 'Wow!' Was all she could say, astounded by the erect vision in front of her.' Come this way.' Will led her by the hand, and as they walked through the archway, Eloise just stood aghast, facing the beautiful sight that was exquisitely breathtaking. 'Wow!' She said once more.

'This is Jacoby's head,' Will pointed out. 'This is one of my favourite walks, it takes you up and over cliffs and down to a white beach.' 'Sounds amazing,' Eloise beamed, with pure excitement in her voice. 'There are some steps to get to the top,' he continued. 'But it isn't high, and they can be avoided if you just want to walk the pathway.' Eloise was aware of the steps and how high it was, but she also knew that she had to somehow conquer her fears now! She had to give it a go, she had to try this, she told herself, and so was happy to mount the steps. She began her trek and was once again astounded by the captivating habitat that stood all around her, teaming with flowers and wildlife, like a huge sanctuary, bursting with colour and fragrances. The air was filled with a beautiful aroma that came from the stunning petals, captivating her as she pushed herself into keeping her legs going, taking each step, eager to reach the top. 'It gets easier, honestly, it does.' Will turned to look at Eloise as she continued to push forward. 'Good job, there are only a few steps, eh!' She added sarcastically. 'Anyway, once you reach the top, it's downhill from there,' Will giggled, looking at her unimpressed face as Spittlebugs crawled in and out of the trees and bushes. Perfectly harmless, so Eloise had been told.

Once at the top, the clifftop walk was a narrow strip pathway, and Eloise was taken aback by the breathtaking view that stood in front of her. Here she was, like she was on top of the world, although feeling excited and in awe, she was still apprehensive and a little anxious. 'Are you okay?' Will asked. 'It is very high, I hope I don't fall,' she answered, overwhelmed. 'Oh, you won't fall here.' Eloise stood silent for a moment, just gazing at Will, waiting for him to crack a smile. He had no reason to tell any porkies, so she thought, especially in this heavenly place. Although heights had never been a favourite of hers, she knew that the more she faced her fears, the more they would be diminished. 'It is true,' he added. 'You cannot fall, as there is no way down, there is nowhere to go, so you would just float.' Eloise's face lit up with a smile as Will took her by the hand, his gesture of making her feel protected, even though in

God's world, everyone is protected and guarded by God, ensuring that they are all safe. The clifftop walk provided a spectacular outlook of the ocean, and along with the white sand that extended as far as the eye could see, it was the most grandiose of views. Eloise was immersed in the tranquillity of heaven as it stretched before her, which created the most magnificent atmosphere she could only ever imagine, and whilst taking in the stunning view, the picture of endlessness fulfilled her with inner peace.

Making her way down the other side, that being a lot easier than walking up, so she had thought, she eyed every step that she took, being careful not to trip. The calming blue water stood just a few feet away now, with its gentle waves invigorating as they gently lapped the shore, whilst pebbles shimmered like crystals in the water. 'Can we sit for a while?' She asked Will. 'Yes, of course.' The beach had always been Eloise's happy place, the smell of the sea always relaxed her, whilst the gentle motion of the waves calmed and soothed her entire body. Removing her sandals, she lay back on the soft sand and closed her eyes as the feeling of paradise filled her body whilst a cool breeze swept over her, leaving a slight tingling to her skin. Taken in by the calm atmosphere that comforted her, as God's glory illuminated off the waves, in an orange hue, she drifted off for a peaceful nap. But no sooner had she dozed off than she was startled by the sound of a flock of seagulls flying overhead. Her eyes flickered as she adjusted to the light, and seeing Will standing beside her, smiling and holding out his hand, she reached out as he tenderly helped her to her feet. In the distance, a line of beach huts caught Eloise's eye, each one made of wood, stood brightly coloured, lending a huge charm to the seafront. Stopping for a second, she picked up a handful of sand, letting each grain sift through her fingers, feeling every little piece of grit as it disappeared to the ground. Her toes buried beneath the warmth of it, at every step she made, and for a split second, she stood still, and breathed in the salty air around her. It was the one place she could admire regularly and never get tired of just staring into this blue lagoon. Hand in hand, Eloise and Will left Jacoby's Head, sure to return to this unspoilt beauty. So many would look upon this place as being just a place to relax, but to Eloise, it was more than that. It was a place of peace and calmness, with a soothing atmosphere that drew you in, and she was sure to return very soon.

Heading to the left, she made her way with Will through yet another woodland, absorbing the tranquillity around her until she came to a flower garden, an oasis of beauty, its hardy blue violets with purple and delicate green stems stood out amongst many other glorious colours. 'You have got to smell this,' Will said, as he gently pulled the flower towards Eloise. She bent close and took a deep breath of the soft blue petals. 'Gracious!' She cried out. 'They are amazing. Such a vibrant fragrance.' Every single flower let out its own distinctive, pleasant aroma, filling the air as she took in the stunning surroundings that stood all around her, and she still could not believe that she was in heaven, for the beauty that she was seeing was something she had only ever dreamt of, yet every step she took was as exquisite as the next. Stopping Eloise in her tracks, Will gently raised her face with his hand, just a little nudge under her chin, and smiled. 'Who would you like to see, if there was one person you really could meet right now?' He asked her, quite sure of what her reply would be. 'Well, that's an obvious answer,' she stated. 'My father, of course,' she added, with no hesitation, as a subtle whistle was heard from behind. 'Dad?' she said, knowing only Kendrick could whistle in that way, and as he turned his daughter around, a beaming smile was upon her face. 'Oh, Dad.' Overcome with emotion, she threw herself into her dad's open arms, being careful not to knock him over as he sniffled. 'My dear daughter.' Eloise consoled him, holding on to him tightly. 'Finally,' she continued. 'I am with you.' She could not believe she was standing in this most beautiful place, in her father's arms. 'Hello, my friend,' said Will, reaching out his arm as he gave a welcoming handshake to the man who was like a father to him. 'Good to see you again, Will,' Kendrick answered, with a firm shake in return. 'I shall leave you two to have some catch-up time, I have a few things to do myself,' Will stated as he kissed his fiancée gently on her cheek and went on his way.

'Let us walk,' Kendrick said, taking his daughter's hand and guiding the way. 'I must show you something.' Eloise looked at her father with a sweet smile, so happy that she was with him.

Kendrick was a tall man; he took after his own father for that and his heart, always full of gentleness and warmth, just like his mother's. His words were always kind, and everyone loved him for that. Eloise had missed spending time with her father and felt guilty that she had not visited him more when he was alive. His passing broke her deeply, and it was something she could not get over, as she believed he had more time. Kendrick had been through so much, especially in his later life, but he was always a fighter and kept on going right until the very end, and Eloise believed that his body could not take any more; he did not have the energy, so he gave up fighting. Now here with him, she was going to make up for lost periods, after all, neither of them were going anywhere, so they had all the moments they could possibly want. As she walked at a gentle pace, the air being crisp, serene, tranquil, and smelling of beautiful blooming flowers, Eloise relished the scents of every one that she could smell. Roses with their soft petals and sweet fragrance were one of many, and as a brightness shimmered in through the gaps in the trees, she continued along the meandering path, as reds, pinks, whites, and yellows stood proud all around. 'Not much further now,' Kendrick piped up, as he carried on walking at his steady pace. Eloise was amazed at the speed he was able to walk, and at times had attempted to try and keep up.

Birds merrily chirped as they flitted from tree to tree, some even gliding to the ground looking for a tasty bite, whilst beautiful butterflies waded throughout the branches that hung gently, their graceful flights and vibrant colours were pleasing to the eye. Kendrick stopped in his path as he scanned his surroundings for a moment. 'Ah,' he paused, 'this way,' and pointing up ahead, he trudged a few more steps until he stopped in his tracks. 'This is Serenity Pool,' he stated, looking directly at his daughter. It was one of many places that Kendrick loved to come to, whether it be to relax or have a gentle swim. 'My word!' Eloise's eyes widened. The pool was an impressive sight to behold, a tranquil oasis, with its crystal-clear water reflecting the vibrant flowers that were positioned within, as a gentle breeze blew. Lush greenery framed the pool like a paradise island, a complex tapestry bursting with a mosaic of textures and tones, whilst an exhibition of ornamental grass stood tall in an array of colours, creating an amazing display, and letting out a sweet scent of vanilla, lemon, and liquorice. 'This is heavenly,' Eloise piped up, as she stood for a moment admiring all that surrounded her, as a brightness cast a warm glow over it, and as the shimmering blue water sparkled, it drew her into its tranquil embrace. 'This is stunning,' she cried.

The poolside provided plush loungers with coloured cushions fitted, a haven for relaxing and resting, beckoning everyone to take a seat, not just Eloise and her father. As Kendrick sat down beside his daughter, palm trees swayed, gently casting dancing shadows on the water's surface as a chorus of birds flew above his head. Eloise's mind wandered for a moment, realising that this was how it was to be from now on. No worries, no pain, no sadness. Just pure love. Their conversation centred on the joys of being there in heaven and how at peace they felt, until Eloise stepped in with a conversation about things she remembered as a child. 'Dad, do you remember the times when you used to build the tents out of your work ladders, planks and dust sheets?' She asked her father and waited patiently for his response. Eloise and her sisters had many moments of fun with these. 'Oh, I do,' Kendrick smiled. 'I also remember the night you chose to camp out in that tent I made you.' 'Oh yes,' Eloise responded with a giggle. She and her sisters were adamant that they would brave it in the dark for one night. 'Only,' said Kendrick. 'You were not in it for very long before running in the back door, screeching!' Eloise could not help chuckling as she remembered that all too well. It had not been much fun, though, being out in the dark and hearing all the strange noises! Kendrick put his arm around his daughter's shoulder and gave her a gentle squeeze as they both laughed together. 'I also remember the walks we went on, Dad, in the woods, and you shouting Snake!' Bellowed Eloise. 'And Lion! A joke, of course,' she said with a smile. 'Ha! Yes,' her father replied. 'But it always made you scream, believing there was one.' 'Yes, and I am sure that is why I became petrified of lions,' she added. 'What about the one about my nose!' Kendrick piped up. Eloise remembered that all too well. 'Oh yes, wasn't that something to do with you trapping it in a door!' 'Well, that is what I told you kids,' He laughed, 'and you believed it.' Both he and Eloise had a good chuckle about it.

Her parents were still together at the time, but later they divorced, whilst Eloise was still quite young. There were many memories Eloise could recall when her parents were still together, but she also made lots of memories with all her stepparents, too. She felt happy spending this time with her father, reminiscing about the old days, but also enjoyed relaxing by the pool, not that there were many people, just a few adults lying back on their sun loungers, feeling quite content, taking in the glorious feel that surrounded them. There was the odd one splashing around in the water, as ripples flowed over their bodies, whilst the pool gave a feel of luxury, serenity and calmness to both Eloise and her father as they sat and watched. 'We must go for a dip next time,' he stated, with a kind smile to his daughter. 'We will for sure, Dad,' she replied hesitantly, for she was never keen on water! 'We will for sure.' 'I must get back now; I have a few seeds to plant, but we will see one another again soon,' Kendrick added, looking down at his daughter smiling, with a twinkle in his eye. His eyes were a subtle blue, but they always seemed to light up when he smiled. 'Yes, Dad, I will see you again, very soon, and we will have that dip in the pool for sure.' Eloise returned the smile and gave her dad a warm hug, then escorted him back in the direction of his home. She had never realised just how much she had missed Kendrick, his voice, his smile, and his kindness, until now. Seeing him again and being with him had been like a dream come true.

CHAPTER 13

Whilst Will was otherwise engaged, and having agreed to meet up later, Eloise chose this moment to take a leisurely stroll by herself as she headed off in the opposite direction to her father, taking in all the heavenly wonder, for around every corner was something different. All through the grounds and in between the trees were crowds of men and women, some with children, older people on their own and some as couples. She enjoyed the peacefulness around her, as birds flittered in and out amongst the people, and branches of the trees stood laden with blossom, being a pleasing sight. Each path was weighted down with white stone and pearls, reflecting light along the way as Eloise took each step, debating on which direction she should take. It was not until now that she had noticed every house had its own name and thought it was a lovely way of giving each one its own unique identity.

Soft pink blush roses with their vibrant petals were exquisite and soothing to her eyes, whilst wildlife could be heard as she walked amongst the sublime trees and flowers, all being a delight to listen to. Butterflies of an assortment of colours, with their velvet wings, landed on the flowers that surrounded her as she sauntered throughout the calm and tranquil woodland, taking in all that nature had to offer, as bright orange leaves fell gently, crunching under her feet as she walked. As a light shone through the gaps between the trees, illuminating the surrounding area, Eloise spotted the pure and calming lake she had briefly been to before with Will, and where she had met Grandma Alicia. It was a picture of sheer perfection even the second time around, she had thought, and like all the lakes here, they were all so soothing and calm. In fact, everywhere in heaven, in her eyes, was so completely flawless that she could not imagine ever being anywhere else, and came to realise that she would not want to be anywhere else, as her eyes continued to take in the pure, picturesque vision that lay in front of her. Stood within the heart of an idyllic meadow and nestled beneath the azure blueness that surrounded her, all seemed to stand still as the golden light filtered through the canopy of the trees with its divine presence of peace and beauty. It was a sight that pleased Eloise, creating an unbelievable pattern on the fresh grass, like individual silk ribbons, as each strand moved in the slight breeze. Lipstick pink tulips adorned the edges of the meadow, the aroma filling the surrounding area with its scent as she nestled herself on a welcoming bench, taking in the glory of not just the breathtaking display of flowers that swayed gently, filling the air with sweet fragrances, but also the silence that surrounded her, giving her the sense of tranquillity. Sitting quietly, all appeared still, and the gold hues which gave off a slight tint shone through the canopied trees as they flickered like tinsel.

It was just a short moment later that half a dozen children arrived, all looking rather cute, their fully pink cheeks complementing their sweet faces and bright smiles, as each one expressed a look of love and awe. 'Oh, my word!' Eloise cried out. 'Carolanne!' She stood up immediately, as she recognised her friend. 'It is you, yes?' Eloise had not seen Carolanne in years, and yet here she was standing upright, glowing, and looking remarkable. 'I cannot believe it,' the woman replied, astounded. 'Eloise?' Her arms outstretched as she welcomed her friend. 'I did not know you were here!' 'I have not been here that long,' answered Eloise as she returned a gentle hug to her old mate. 'Come and join us,' Carolanne said, shaking out the huge picnic mat on the plush green grass, trying in vain not to cover the daisies, although it was an impossible task, being that they were everywhere. As Eloise sat down on the warm, cosy blanket, the children, who looked between three and seven, huddled in beside her, just staring, and smiling, making her feel as though she was their best friend, and she liked that. 'Who are all these children?' She asked. Carolanne looked up whilst emptying the picnic basket of its contents of homemade treats and fruit. 'They are some of the children who have come to this glorious land, but have no mum or dad here.' She went on. 'Oh, it seems sad to think they have no parents here,' replied Eloise, unwrapping the sandwiches and handing them out to each child, with a piece of fruit. 'They are not alone, they are not aware of that state of being, neither do they know of sadness, for God takes care of them,' Carolanne added. 'He is their family; he protects them and watches them flourish. The children are all very happy.' 'That is lovely to know, and what a better way to bond with one another than to have a picnic filled with joy in this most natural setting. I would love to help in any way I can,' she added. 'We have many woodland activities with the children, perhaps you would care to come along with us when we finish here before I take the children back.' Carolanne poured some fresh juice into each of the children's cups and handed it to them, whilst Eloise collected a few daisies and linked them together one by one. As the children watched in amazement, one girl did not hesitate to speak out. 'What are you making?' She asked in the sweetest of voices. 'A daisy chain,' Eloise answered, as she gently tied the bracelet of daisies around the little girl's wrist. The rest of the children were quick on the mark to hold out their wrists as they waited patiently for Eloise to make one for each of them. 'You've made some friends there,' piped up Carolanne. Eloise smiled, feeling grateful for how quickly the children had taken to her.

Vibrant colours of scented flowers and lush green grass filled Eloise's senses with delight as she enjoyed the company that was around her. She had got to know Carolanne many years before, but sadly, after they had both moved away to different areas, they lost touch. But Eloise had always wondered what had happened to her dear friend!

After gathering everything up, she and Carolanne took the children on a gentle walk, inspiring them and sparking their imagination as they spotted a variety of birds flying throughout the trees, each child calling out the names of every bird. 'Woodpecker, chaffinch, golden crest, yellow hammer.' The names seemed to just roll off the children's tongues without hesitation. 'Wow!' Eloise remarked, totally impressed, as she collected up a small bundle of branches and sticks. 'The children here learn so much,' piped up Carolanne. 'We educate them on the importance of nature and teach them how to be kind and show them how to plant flowers and how to look after them, as well as art projects with leaves and twigs,' she added. 'It is pretty important, I guess,' replied Eloise, as she wedged the branches she had collected into a tree to create her framework and began to build a den, as the children helped to collect twigs and leaves to fill the gaps, making walls. Seeing them smile and laugh, and feeling that she was being of some help, made Eloise's heart fill with happiness, as one by one, they entered the finished den. All around the woodland were different groups of children, some making dens, some playing catch, and others just sitting and chatting. A beautiful sight to see. 'You must come again,' said Carolanne. 'Help out anytime, we will always be grateful for the company, and the children will love seeing you.' 'Yes, I will be sure to do that, it will be lovely to see you all again.' She bid farewell to her friend and children and made her way back to the water, reflecting on the time she had spent with them.

Radiant light soaked the lake with its beauty as nearby rabbits scampered across Eloise's vision in a flash. She could not get her head around just how beautiful it all was, and loved the fact that she could return any time to this place of peaceful calmness. No sounds ran out from the shimmering emptiness of the space around her; it was as if she were in this glorious place, alone, as she sat and thought for a moment of all that had happened since she had arrived in beautiful heaven. As she took in all the glorious wonder that she was so grateful for, and all the wonderful people she had happily chatted to, and members of her family she had met, she closed her eyes and bowed her head gently to one side.

Unaware of how long it had been, Eloise jumped suddenly into Will's hand, stroking her face. 'Sorry, did I startle you?' 'Oh, just a little,' she answered, sitting upright. 'How was your walk, my love?' 'Oh, very enjoyable,' she answered as she filled him in on all that she had done and seen. 'Are you feeling at home here in heaven, and settled?' Eloise was surprised that Will felt he even had to ask that. 'This is my home now,' she responded. 'Oh, good.' Will nodded in affirmation, as they sat quietly for a moment, Eloise resting her head gently on his shoulder, it being the perfect atmosphere to drift off to sleep again; however, she knew that she would regret it, for she would miss all the precious beauty that stood before her, as colours of red, orange, and yellow filled the air. Whilst the water was calm and beautiful in every aspect, as it swirled in its gentle motion, Eloise chose to just sit and stare, as she admired and cherished it like a picture in a frame.

'Would you like to go in one of those rowing boats with me?' Will asked suddenly, as he sharply rose to his feet. Eloise was startled, for she believed she may have nodded off again! She had not spotted the boats before, yet here stood several, as she observed closely, feasting her eyes on every one that sat at the bank of the lake. Ultramarine blues and whites sat proudly; each one tied up with their oars lying loosely inside. ''Errrrrrrrmmmm…' she paused for a second. Ermmmmmm,' she sighed once more. 'You will be okay,' Will reassured her. 'Ohhhhhhh,' she answered, uncertain as to whether she was making the right decision. Stepping into the boat, helped by Will, Eloise hesitated for a moment, in fear of falling into the water. She had never been keen on boats or water after nearly drowning as a teenager in the sea, and it had put the fear up her ever since. Clinging on to the sides with a tight grip, Will clambered in, rocking the boat more than she had done herself. 'I am guessing you know how to row a boat?' She asked, trying to take her mind off how she was feeling. 'Not really,' was Will's doubtful answer. 'But how difficult can it be,' he laughed, trying to fathom out how to hold the oars, but it was not long before he had eventually got the idea of it, even if they spent most of the time going around in circles, but Eloise was grateful for the calm and quiet lake, the surroundings overwhelmingly peaceful, as Will rowed gently, and the fact that nobody else was about for her to feel embarrassed was a bonus. Putting the oars to one side, Will sat looking at Eloise for a moment. Her hair hung gently as a soft breeze blew, whilst her dreamy brown eyes gleamed. She looked as she had always looked, beautiful, and Will was so glad that she was with him again. All was quiet for a moment until Eloise realised that he was watching her! 'Why are you looking at me like that?' She asked, smiling. 'Because you are so beautiful, and I love you.' 'I love you too,' she replied, feeling a little more at ease now he was not rowing. They spent the time catching up on the events that happened leading up to Will's final moments before he passed. 'Did you feel alone?' She asked, straight out. 'When you passed away, I mean, because I stayed with you all day, yet it was like you knew you were going,' she went on. 'You were so tired, yet you would not sleep while I was there. Why?' As Will took Eloise's hand in his, he looked at her and patted it gently. 'I think I knew that my time was coming to an end, but I did not want to go while you were still with me. Even though I could not take any more, I waited until you had left that day. What happened to me was for the best. I did not want to have to live with more pain or with how I ended up as, because it would not have been a life for

106

me or for us. So, I waited until you left, and I remember just closing my eyes,' he continued. 'It was so peaceful. I felt so calm and relaxed, I was not scared,' he added. 'I am sorry, my love.' Eloise hugged him gently. 'It is okay, I understand. I would never have wanted you to keep suffering,' she added. 'I am here now, darling. We are together again now,' she smiled.

The cool air swept Eloise's hair back behind her ears as the boat slowly glided upon the water, Will directing them towards the mooring edge. No more crippling thoughts occurred; in fact, she became less and less afraid of falling out and discovered that all the years she had been scared, she never had the opportunity to face the distress she was living with, until now. As Will helped her out of the boat, for a moment, she lost herself in the reflection of what she saw in the water. Orange rays had turned the lake into a bright sheet of gold, creating a stunning display of pure beauty, a sight to behold.

The day had been yet another eventful one of great joy, and Eloise felt happiness fulfil her inside like every moment that she had spent in beautiful heaven so far. Shutting the blinds in the room to block out the light, she laid herself down on the bed and closed her eyes, as she thought about all that had happened since she had been in this glorious place, as well as conquering all her fears and worries. From the second she had entered the elegant gates, to seeing the picturesque surroundings of golden tranquillity, she knew she was where she was meant to be. Although unaware of time in heaven, she understood that it had been a while since she had arrived in this perfect place. Having the most beautiful house in surroundings she could only ever imagine and meeting all those that have always been so close to her, and she looked forward to seeing all those that were to come to this incredible place at some point, and she knew that they too would be happy and at peace, just the same as her.

CHAPTER 14

Vibrant rays shone through the blinds in the room, waking Eloise, as her father stood before her. Waking up for her had always been an easy task, as she had always been a morning person, plus, why would she want to miss out on all the beauty that was around her? 'Where is Will?' She asked, pushing her neck into her luxurious pillow, loving the feel of its loose, fluffy clusters. 'He has had to go and sort a few things for someone, so I thought I could take you to see some more of this wonderland. I have an idea of somewhere that you will really love to see, is that okay?' 'Oh yes, Dad, that will be lovely,' she replied, stretching her arms above her head, yawning. She rose to her feet sharpish, intrigued as to where they would be going, although she really did not mind, as just spending quality time with her father was more than enough. Something she had not had when they were both alive. Another exquisite view stood before her eyes as she walked amongst the pure serenity of what lay ahead of her and Kendrick, and whilst the peace and quiet that surrounded her was soul soothing, she found that the beauty in all the colours of every flower she passed was spellbinding. As trees parted, the smell of refreshing scents followed her as twigs crunched under her feet, breaking the silence at every step she made, whilst a golden ore that shone in the distance cast an extra light, which helped guide her, although unaware of what direction! She had left that to her father.

A bright red iron gate stood in all its grandeur in front of Eloise, as vibrant hues of flowers with their velvet petals hung softly around the outside of it. Clematis, the queen of climbers, roses and sweet peas were just a few that stood on display, each one letting out an incredible aroma. As she nudged the gate open, it creaked with every little push that she gave it, and although she had no idea what was on the other side, she was curious. Whilst Kendrick stood aside, letting his daughter walk in first, squirrel's bushy tails twitched as they scurried between the railings, whereas Eloise stood in awe at the breathtaking sight, barely able to speak. 'Goodness!' Was all she could manage, as she tried to take in all that stood in front of her now. It was like she was walking into a sanctuary of peace and beauty, she thought, as she was immediately soothed by the trees as they swayed gently, each one providing a shelter to sit under if she wanted to just lie back and take in the serenity of the nature that enveloped her.

'This is the Garden of Saint Peter,' Kendrick told her. Eloise was immediately struck by the eye-catching colours of the perfectly manicured shrubs and flowers that stood around her, and she could already smell the sweet fragrances. Rows and rows of beds lay beautifully, with their vibrant flowers standing proud, as each one was neatly arranged, and every clump was thriving. A fountain caught Eloise's eye as it stood tall on its black concrete base in all its glory, adding to the picturesque scenery of the garden. Its crystal-clear water cascading over, dropping onto small stones below, as white, pink, purple and yellows sparkled in the light. Each ripple formed a peaceful harmony, as sprays danced in a smooth and graceful way in the fountain, leaving Eloise feeling illuminated within every crevice of her soul. Both she and her father stopped in their tracks as Kendrick turned to his daughter with a smile, 'Between 15000 and 35000 species of flowers here,' he explained. 'A lot of them have the tiniest seeds ever, with just a single one having up to three million seeds inside it.' Eloise, with her mouth wide open, was astounded as she continued to take in all that stood within this exotic beauty with its exhibition of stunning flowers. She was fascinated by all that she saw and was keen to walk further along the path, as the scent from each individual flower soon made her surroundings a fragrant paradise. Rows and rows of wooden benches stood along the path from the fountain, and Eloise was not surprised at the amount of people who were sitting on them as she stood quietly for a moment, whilst looking at the scenery that was so peaceful and serene. In conclusion, where she was standing right now was an immense oasis of nature, as birds sang, butterflies flitted from flower to flower, whilst their delicate wings shimmered in the light. Mixed flowers with their beautiful scents filled this delightful garden with outstanding colour, and combined with the tranquillity of the mesmerising experience Eloise was having right now, made her feel totally refreshed. She did not want to leave, as was quite taken with all that she was seeing, and it meant a lot to her, for it was more than just a garden. It was a space that brought everyone together, offering a great sense of peace, with every scent here, letting out a gentle and sweet smell. As her father called her, she knew they had to be on their way, and whilst the light shone brightly down on them both as they left the beautiful garden, Eloise was grateful for all that she had seen. 'Thank you, Dad.' Eloise turned and looked at her father as she hugged him lightly. 'That really was a magnificent place, somewhere I shall surely go back to,' she said with delight, and as thoughts of comfort filled her head, she realised that the garden would await her until next time when she was to pass this way again.

They walked now, at a slow pace, Eloise unaware of where her father was taking her next! 'I wish to take you to my home as you have not seen it yet,' said Kendrick. 'Is that okay?' He added 'I cannot wait,' answered Eloise, knowing it would be a stunning house as her dad would have decorated it all himself. The ground curved gently with an array of stunning flowers standing upright in every direction Eloise looked. Purples, crimson, oranges, and the brightest yellows her eyes had ever seen, each display was breathtaking with panoramic views in every step she took in this captivating land. She could not believe the nature she had surveyed up to now. Baby ducklings waddled, following their confident mother, to find the nearest water, as birds chirped, calling each other in the cool air, as twigs snapped underneath them, whilst squirrels chased one another up and down trees. Eloise was grateful for this precious place that God had let her be in, for seeing all her loved ones, for the sweet sounds, leisurely strolls and appreciating all that the scenery had to offer, and observing all the plants and nature and the tranquillity of it all. She had been blessed with this peaceful place that was now home.

A golden light cast upon the surrounding area, spreading over the whole of heaven with its streaks of pink and oranges as Kendrick and his daughter proceeded a little further, until they soon reached a charming little cottage, situated on the edge of the Garden of Saint Peter. Eloise had come to realise that the houses in heaven were from all different eras- some modern and huge, and some cottages that were rather quaint, but, even so, they were all extremely beautiful and peaceful, and she was filled with wonder and delight as she walked up to her father's home. Whilst a small hedge was being hugged by a variety of rose bushes, a mixture of reds, yellows, and pinks, the cottage itself could still be seen. Although it had an old look about it, it still had charm and character, which made it stand out from any of the other cottages Eloise had seen before. Whilst its quaint path of rustic charm led to an oak door with elegant panelling, a variety of baskets hung, each one filled with an array of mixed flowers. Violets with their large, heart-shaped leaves and petals in purple, displayed in one, whilst lavender stood positioned upright in another. Petunias, with their wide, trumpet-shaped flowers of all colours, and branching foliage, stood bright and lively in the remainder of the baskets. 'This is Rose Cottage,' Kendrick smiled. 'It is beautiful, Dad. You always did love your flowers.' Eloise smiled back at her father as he led the way into his home.

The hallway felt warm and inviting, characterised by a comfortable and relaxed appearance of pastel colours on the walls, creating a serene and gentle atmosphere. A small, patterned rug added warmth and texture to the natural wood flooring, but also made it soothing on one's feet. As Eloise walked on, into the lounge, she was adorned with love, comfort, and welcoming memories as she took in all that filled this quaint room. From its small, latticed windows to the yellow rose that stood proud, letting off its sweet fragrance, to the family photos that were displayed on each wall. A dark green shaggy rug lay scattered on the wood floor, which added comfort to the room, whilst the two two-seaters, with their softness and laid-back feel, were just what Eloise expected, and were something that Kendrick cherished too. The narrow hall from the lounge was a slender passage where the stairs fitted in perfectly, leading to three fair-sized bedrooms, one of which was being used as her father's sketching and painting gallery, his much-loved hobby. The compact kitchen was amicable, and Kendrick had incorporated functional storage, making the most of the available space, whilst still being cosy and efficient for all his needs. Her father had always taken it upon himself to ensure his home was given a unique touch by his own gentle hands, with a fresh coat of paint on a regular basis, and despite being a small cottage, the light reflecting colour of white and a pale shade of grey on the walls seemed to enhance the space even more. 'Come,' Kendrick said, as he led the way. 'I have something to show you.' A marbled terrace joined the back of the cottage, leading on to a grassed area. A small but compact space, with its array of vibrant flowers of all kinds, stood neatly positioned beside fruit trees, laden with every possible fruit. 'This is exquisite, Dad,' Eloise expressed. Her eyes were trying to take in every detail of every colour that surrounded her. 'Let us sit down for a while,' Kendrick suggested as he guided his daughter to a wooden bench that he had made himself. Light in colour, almost a pine, covered with a soft cushion, making it feel very welcoming. It had a warmth about it, Eloise thought, as she sat herself down on the cosy seat, content as she took in the surrounding glory that flowed around her. Kendrick sat beside her, just as golden rays cast a warm glow upon the peaceful cottage, and a sense of calmness radiated an air of serenity. Just at that moment, a fox appeared at the bottom of the garden. 'Oh, would you look at that,' cried Eloise, as she watched a little fox eating berries and fruit from a plastic dish, supposedly left by Kendrick. 'That is my little friend, he comes here often.' 'He is the tamest fox I have ever seen,' Eloise added. She believed it was the same fox that had always visited Kendrick when he was alive!

It was at that moment that she watched her father, as a smile lit up his face, and she knew then that he was happy and completely settled in this place of peace and joy. 'Dad,' she whispered, just as Kendrick turned to face his daughter. 'There are so many things I never got to say to you before, like, just how much I have always loved you.' She smiled. 'Oh, my dearest daughter,' he said with a comforting tone to his voice. 'I know how much you have always loved me, right from a child,' he spoke. 'But,' cried Eloise. 'I never told you enough. Especially growing up, I never said enough times how much I love you or how grateful I was to you for all you ever did for me.' 'I knew,' answered her father. 'I knew you loved me as much as I have always loved you, Eloise, the same as I have always cared about you.' Normally, by now, she would have tears running down her cheeks, but it did not feel strange either, because she knew there were no tears in heaven, so instead, Eloise hugged her father. 'You were always such a great dad, but I never told you.' She continued. 'You did so much for me and always supported me with everything and believed in me. Thank you, Dad.' She smiled, giving Kendrick another huge hug, just as he wrapped his arms around his daughter's waist and gently hugged her back. 'And thank you, Dad, for all the times you were there for me, I never showed you or told you how I appreciated that so much.' Kendrick was and always had been Eloise's pillar of strength. The greatest man she knew, and she was always amazed at his dedication to working, putting everything into it. Every adventure with her dad meant having fun and making memories, and she certainly had a lot of that in her previous life, growing up. Kendrick was never really one for showing his feelings; rather, he was a laid-back kind of man, but when it came to being a gentleman, he was the one, with his warm smile and kind eyes. Eloise had always loved his smile because it always lit up a room, wherever he was, and always made everyone else smile. She was always so grateful that this man was her dad.

There was no measurement of time in heaven, but what seemed like a fair while of sitting chatting in her father's home, Eloise was ready to make her way, as much as she enjoyed catching up with him. She hugged her dad gently and thanked him for the glorious moment she had spent with him, grateful for a much-needed catch-up. 'It has been a day of such wonder, my dearest daughter.' Kendrick returned the hug, and as Eloise smiled and slowly walked away, she could not help but look back over her shoulder and drop another smile towards him.

CHAPTER 15

Whilst taking in the refreshing cool breeze that gently brushed against her face, hues of flowers with their striking green foliage and vibrant colours created a beautiful tapestry that was pleasing to her eye. It felt good walking through every piece of woodland that connected her to nature, as she felt comfort in all its serene beauty.

A stunning dome-shaped abbey stood positioned tall and proud, leaving Eloise open-mouthed with the beauty it gave out, as it took her breath away for a second. Its visually striking features, that being bricks of rustic beige, filled golden pillars on either side, as golden railings encircled the entire building, whilst strands of grass, like silken threads, waved in the cool breeze. It was the crystal glass windows and arched entrance of the same shade that gave the abbey its finishing touch, as the pillars gave it its overall look of welcoming all. A sound of beautiful voices like angels came from inside as Eloise entered the abbey, and she sensed a feeling of calmness and relaxation as Peter welcomed her with a gentle word of prayer. She was not only hypnotised by the detail of every pew that sat before her, but also the captivating fountain that took her into a realm of what felt like a symphony of tranquillity, as it stood with its array of vibrant colours of lush foliage around it, that bloomed from each flower, almost taking her breath away. What a beautiful thing to have in an abbey, she thought, as the gorgeous fountain stood in its surroundings, letting out soothing sounds of flowing water whilst it trickled down, creating a serene feeling of calmness whilst ensuring a relaxing atmosphere. The peacefulness and tranquil feeling Eloise had was extremely surprising.

There were so many people in the abbey, not what she was expecting at all, but it was a place that everyone came to whenever they wished. There was not a particular service, for here it was where everyone was welcomed at any moment; they could just show up. Peter liked to wait a while just to see if more were to arrive, although he welcomed people at every moment and was always ready to listen if they wanted to speak with him. As a choir of children stood singing, a brightness came through the windows, lighting up every corner of the abbey. Just then, Eloise spotted her stepfather sitting at one of the pews. 'Hello Eli,' she said, with a gentle smile, as she sat down beside him. Although the pews were made from sturdy oak wood, Eloise was grateful for the padded cushions that added a little comfort. 'Hello,' Eli whispered as they sat back and enjoyed listening to the harmonious voices of the choir of youngsters.

Peter made everyone feel welcome after the children had finished their hymn, and the abbey stood silent for a moment, until.... 'To all and one, to those that have been here for some while and to those that have not long arrived here in this beautiful land.' He went on, as he smiled towards Eloise. 'God. The Father, Son, and Holy Spirit. He is 'one.' He who cares for his creation, who spreads teachings, who guides us. He who forgives our sins.' Peter paused. 'The discussion I would like to share with you all at this moment is 'forgiveness.' He went on. 'Forgiveness does not mean you stop hurting,' again, he looked up at Eloise! 'But, if you hold on to any kind of evilness that someone has done to you, it will weigh you down. You must learn,' he continued. 'That if you forgive those who have hurt you, the Lord will forgive you if you do something wrong.' Eloise felt a comforting warmth within her body at what Peter was saying right now. That forgiveness was an essential concept, and it meant she needed to let go of all the hatred and anger she was holding inside for the person who had previously destroyed her. She understood now that it was the only way anyone could move forward, and that was to not keep holding on to the past. No more holding grudges. This was where Eloise had to free herself. It was all making complete sense, and what better place to do it than where she was right now?

After listening to several hymns that the children sang gracefully within the abbey walls, Peter finished with a prayer in which Eloise, amongst others, ended with an Amen. He then bid farewell to her, and as he smiled, he clasped her hand in his, giving it a gentle pat. 'Know that you can speak with me at any moment you wish to, whether it be in the abbey here or when you see me around talking with others, and know that you can talk to God at any moment you feel the need.

He is present, he is always around you.' Eloise returned his smile, 'Thank you,' she replied, grateful that she was where she was, for heaven was her world.

Bells began to ring as Eloise walked across the courtyard of the abbey with her stepfather, and she was immediately struck by a rich aroma of coffee as it wafted up. 'Mmmmmmmmmm, that smells good,' she remarked, following Eli into a small room, where four tables and a selection of brown vintage chairs stood, amicable for the cosy space that she was looking at right now. The ceiling, made of glass, was the perfect way of filling this area with natural light, so she thought, and a cute little book corner, with its narrow shelf, displayed an assortment of Bibles and prayer books, made to welcome anyone who wished to come along for a quiet read. 'What a sweet little space this is,' Eloise piped up once more. 'I shall definitely have many a quiet moment sat here.' She turned and faced Eli with a cheerful smile. The approach to the garden was a truly unique space, so Eloise thought, with an oasis of greenery that encircled the area. 'Oh, how beautiful is this,' she said, looking at what filled the space in front of her. 'This is the Eternal Garden,' Eli stated. 'It has an undercover section and outdoor space for people to come and just basically enjoy, or to sit and say a few prayers if they wish to, or you can just take in all the glorious space around you.' 'What a beautiful idea,' she piped up, taking in all that surrounded her, as she continued her walk down the cobblestone path, lined with rows of trees that stood tall, whilst their robust branches hung gently and chestnut brown sparrows with their contrasting black cheek spots, flew from one tree canopy to another. The garden had been shaped beautifully, with its long and narrow path curving the full length of the abbey, and everywhere that Eloise looked, hanging from the trees, were the most succulent fruits, their skins unblemished as they hung daintily from the branches. Clusters of rosy, red apples, perfect peaches, and tantalising oranges. The garden was surrounded by pots and pots of fragrant flowers and sounds of wind chimes as they let out their melodious tunes, which Eloise found to be quite charming. The garden had a few beautiful sections, including a tulip courtyard and a rose garden filled with the most amazing scents coming from each plant, whilst comfy seating provided a resting place for every passerby. 'It is so important, having this,' Eli gestured widely. 'A tranquil space for reflection, relaxing, and a connection with the abbey itself, for it teaches us so much about ourselves and about our relationship with God, but it also brings together so many who also have a passion for nature.' 'I couldn't have put it better myself,' Eloise answered, grateful for the abbey and its garden and having that sense of belonging and support. They continued their walk for just a short while longer, and as hymns of praise were sung, Eloise bid farewell to her stepfather, giving him a gentle hug. 'I am so grateful that you have shown me this,' she stated. 'For I believe that this garden is a sanctuary where we can experience joy in worshipping together, but also, having alone time with God. I am so grateful for his guidance, which has uplifted me and comforted me.' Eli returned the hug to his stepdaughter and bid farewell for the time being. There seemed to be so much scenery that Eloise found she had not spotted before, and so many more houses that sat in amongst the stunning grounds, each one being surrounded by a vast amount of beauty and having its own personality. As she made her way back to the lake with the waterfall, her favourite place by far, she had the same thoughts again, of happiness, and feelings of calmness, because she was in a place where nothing mattered, where there were no worries, just love, joy and everlasting peace.

It was only a short distance ahead until she could see the brightness of the light that reflected off the falling water, and the sight was spectacular as she drew closer, feeling as though she was in paradise. It would not have mattered how many times she saw this; she knew it would look better each time, even the Atlantic blue water looked the clearest she had seen, and she did not think she could ever take her eyes off it. It was like looking through a piece of glass as the stunning display of cascading water that was crystal clear and captivating, plunged down the rocks into a clear lake at the bottom. It was just so beautiful, and Eloise had never seen a scene as breathtaking as the one she was seeing right now, as the splashing of the water shimmered against the rocks, and even though it made some noise, the sheer look of what sat in front of her made up for her ears shattering. Waves of white plunged over the rocks as they foamed at the bottom, and even as loud as they were, she felt it was soothing in an unusual way. Bewildered to, as the surge of water cast oneself into the pool below, as the heavenly, leaking light added a golden tint to the face of it. Paradise was what came to Eloise's mind as it reflected off the falling water, and as a lather of foam fell, she could feel the coolness of it as it splashed against her skin. Entranced by the beauty of it all and feeling the fresh air, she stood still for a moment and reflected upon all that she was seeing in front of her, as sprays from the fountain tippled over her arms, making her feel a little chillier than normal, but she did not feel disappointed as the glorious sight made up for that. As she walked away, the softness of the grass beneath her feet tickled her toes through her sandals, and the sweet aroma of the flowers that stood around her filled the air. Thankful for the shimmering light that reflected off the downpour from the waterfall, it made it a safe, quiet atmosphere, unlike anything she had ever experienced before, and she felt so happy to be standing where she was.

CHAPTER 16

Even though she preferred to stay, she managed to tear herself away from the glorious sight that surrounded her and took a leisurely stroll amongst the cosy canopy of welcoming trees. Whilst the softness of the woodland under her feet gave her a spring in her step, she thought about all that had occurred since her arrival in heaven, from her entrance to now and could not believe just how much had happened and wondered what more was to follow. Grateful to all that she had in this beautiful place, but also all that she was learning, not just about here in heaven, but about herself, too.

A vast number of twisted branches hummed with life all around her, as an enchanting symphony of colour greeted her at every step she made, and the air, filled with a magnificent aroma of flowers, let out a sweet-smelling scent intoxicating her surroundings as she walked. Once through the trees, she was immediately wowed by the most beautiful golden bridge she had ever set her eyes on, and as the light shone down on it, every part of it sparkled, unlike anything she had ever witnessed before. As beautiful as it was, Eloise was unable to estimate how long or how high the bridge was, as there is not a single, defined length or height for a bridge in heaven, although, saying that, it was VERY high, and VERY long, and it was at that moment, the nerves suddenly got the better of her. She could just about see Will, waiting on the other side of the bridge, in his usual relaxed manner, looking his normal handsome self, smiling, and waving. She smiled back, giving a nervous wave in return, wondering how she was going to achieve this!

Flowers of all colours stood positioned upright amongst the freshly cut grass that surrounded the golden bridge. Lilies, with their flamboyant trumpet petals, cotton candy-tinted hybrids with their nodding flowers and layers of ruffles inside, displayed an assortment of colours. Oranges and yellows stood proudly in clumps, allowing everyone that passed by to see these beauties, whilst violet pansies with their oval shape and serrated edges sat neatly amongst the surrounding array of flowers. Soft-feathered ducklings bobbed up and down as they followed their confident mother, quacking as they gently swayed underneath the bridge, whilst bright orange fish swam in and out amongst the ducklings, as one by one they continued to waddle behind their mother, as she moved in a different direction.

'I do not have to walk over that, do I?' Eloise shouted out to Will, feeling a little on edge. She had always been petrified of heights, and right now had that same feeling she had always got, that her insides were about to leap from her stomach. She supposed that Will was probably thinking, Go on, girl, you can do this! 'It will be okay,' he shouted in her direction. But she was not so sure! She trembled and panicked, and instead of a strong urge of wanting to escape the situation, it left her frozen on the spot, even though she knew she had to somehow make her way across the bridge to meet him. 'I do not know if I can. I am not sure if I am up for this one bit.' 'Take a few steps, then you will see it is okay. Have faith in God, my love. Do not stop, just keep moving forward.' 'Come on, you can do this,' Eloise said to herself. 'You are a capable woman.'

As she began to walk slowly across the bridge, her nerves began building within her, but there was nothing she could do, apart from attempting another step, knowing she only had to make it to the other side and she would be okay. 'Don't look down,' she kept telling herself, and even though she was unable to see if there was a huge drop below her, something inside her immediately made her feel that she had no fear. It was as though she had this sudden connection, as a sense of tranquillity gently warmed her body. Keeping her head held high, she took a step at a time until she finally reached the halfway mark, feeling increasingly comfortable with each step, then another deep breath and another step, until she finally reached the other side, grateful for Will's hand that reached out, taking hers in his. 'See, I knew you could do it,' Will praised her with a huge hug. 'Yes, I did, didn't I?' Eloise replied, still feeling a little shaken, but proud of herself for conquering her fear, as a soothing atmosphere filled her with a sheer embrace as she stepped off the bridge. Eloise stood still for a moment, her mouth wide open, for she was totally lost for words. There in front of her was an array of vibrant colours that lay stretched as far as the eye could see, and it was not long before she had forgotten about the trauma of the bridge.

It was no garden. Rather a landscape of tranquillity as she took in the glorious acres of grassland with its assortment of flowers. Beautiful and vibrant colours in a variety of tints caught her eye, as lilac and yellow buttercups and cowslips stood rubbing shoulders together, whilst powder blue orchids stunned her, as they stood mixed in amongst the grasses, and in the distance, stood a mountain of rocks, coloured ones at that, something Eloise had never witnessed before. 'Wow!' She cried, excitedly, her eyes almost bursting from their sockets. 'This is stunning.' She smiled as she breathed in the sweet smell that filled the air. 'This is Rainbow Valley,' Will replied. Hundreds of rocks stood proud in their awe-inspiring wonder of colours as they integrated within one another, and Eloise began to feel like a merry-go-round from all the spinning, as she took in all its grandeur and resplendent beauty, whilst experiencing a sense of admiration. 'Simply sublime,' she smiled, as she stood still in a moment of thought. 'I have never seen anything so glorious with such lush colours,' she added as the heavenly light illuminated the sea of colour between the flowers and the rocks, and as she was drawn to the enchanting embrace of them, they drew her in closer. Grasshoppers chirped piercingly as butterflies fluttered in amongst the shades of lavenders and oranges of the flowers, flapping their wings, gliding from grass to grass. 'Do you wish to climb the rocks and have a look from the top?' Whispered Will, as he stroked Eloise's brow. 'Mind you, it is very high.' 'Oh, if I can manage that bridge, I am sure I will be able to manage a few steps and conquer the height of the rocks,' Eloise replied in a positive manner and with that, she set forth with Will in tow and mounted the coloured steps, one by one, as she took in all the gloriousness as she climbed, and although there was plenty to admire, as she clambered to the top, it was where she was fulfilled with the most beautiful views of entire heaven. The scenery was simply gorgeous, and as it captivated Eloise's heart and mind, it was only then that she appreciated all that she had been given in this glorious place, a picturesque, lush landscape of undulating bliss. After what seemed like a lengthy duration, she made her way across, following Will, as she continued to take in the stunning views along the way, and once on the other side, she was able to carefully move forward, down the coloured steps and sit for a while on a nearby bench taking in the cool breeze that blew gently across the valley. It was only a short moment after, that a group of people headed towards Eloise, and she immediately recognised a couple of faces, each one looking smart, dressed in their white robes, whilst every sash was tied loosely around their waist. The closer they became, the more people she recognised, as they each smiled at her, and the one that she feasted her eyes upon first was the woman up front. Jana, with her once hunched body, now stood upright, and her hair that for so long was a smoky grey, now shone bright as it hung beautifully, sweeping against her silky skin, and resting upon her shoulders. Her once gaunt frame was now a straight posture. 'Hello Eloise, do you remember me?' The sweet woman gave a pleasant smile as she walked towards Eloise, then held out her hand. 'Yes,' she cried out. 'Aunty Jana,' she answered as she took her by the hand, and with the other gave her a gentle hug. Jana, Kendrick's sister, was always the strong one in the family, and at 92 when she passed, no one was surprised that she had lived so long. Renske, slightly hidden behind Jana, was her husband, who had passed away several years before. His once unsteady limp was now an upright and strong steady stance as he walked forward and hugged Eloise. Several more faces were recognised by her, including those of her uncles and cousins who had passed away many years before. Rosemary, whom Eloise had seen briefly when she first arrived in heaven, stepped forward. 'Hello again, dear,' she said as she leaned in for a gentle squeeze. 'You look so well,' Eloise whispered, returning the hug. As a child, she used to love living next door to Rosemary and her black Labrador Jake, and she had often wondered what happened to this beautiful lady; now here she was.

Eloise recognised so many more people within the group as she chatted to each person that stood before her, and as she worked her way through the crowd, she immediately spotted a face that she had never forgotten. That of her uncle Terrick, her mother's brother. As he slowly inched his way forward, Eloise reached out and placed her arms around his small frame and squeezed him gently, being careful not to hurt him. He was always a delicate man, not weak, just fragile, but Eloise was rather shocked at how strong he was at managing to hold himself up. In fact, she could not get over how different everyone seemed, for they all had such strength and great postures and skin, the smoothest she had ever seen. Heaven was certainly doing something for all that had arrived in this magnificent place.

'Eloise, my dearest one, so good to see you here.' 'Oh, uncle,' Eloise replied. 'I am so happy to be here with you. I was so sad when you departed, and I never got to say goodbye to you.' Terrick was Eloise's favourite uncle, not that she ever admitted it to anyone in the family, but she always felt that she had such a connection with him, maybe because they both loved to write! She loved that Terrick was the gentlest of men and had the kindest and warmest of hearts and the softest voice that would make anyone feel at ease. 'We are here together now,' Terrick spoke out. 'No need to be sad anymore.' He gave another hug to Eloise and a pleasant smile as his eyes twinkled. 'You are a precious one that has been sent here to cherish all that awaits you. Except it all, Eloise, this is your home now.' 'Yes, yes, I will, uncle,' she returned his hug.

Lots of smiles stood before her, and she was so happy to see all the people that she had not seen for many years, all so welcoming and kind as they told her of their lives in heaven and how they had come to be there. Eloise had been moved by their strength and courage and enjoyed catching up with everyone, and for what seemed like a long while after, she and Will bid farewell for the time being, giving gentle hugs all around as they made their way back to their home. Eloise loved all that she was seeing in heaven, and every beautiful sight did not hang back in putting a smile upon her face.

CHAPTER 17

As she silently walked away from the crowd, their chattering in the distance became quieter, and Eloise started reflecting on all those that she had seen and spoken to, feeling amazed by the awesome beauty that surrounded her. As she and Will made their way through high-stretched trees, their twisted branches with expanded fingers directed them on their path as a thick carpet of leaves crunched beneath every footstep that they made. A deer ran past quickly, which made Eloise jump in mid-air, and as she slid to the ground, a sense of awe filled her as a slight breeze bustled its way amongst the canopied trees. As Will kindly helped her up, a small, agile lady stood before her, and Eloise immediately recognised her as she threw herself into her nan's arms and gave her a huge hug. 'Nan,' she cried out. Bea's smile was worth more than any words, so Eloise thought. 'Welcome home,' Bea whispered, and gave her granddaughter a warm hug in return.

Bea was Eloise's mum's mum, who had been gone for many years. A small lady with a dainty, round face, her eyes prominent and her short hair had a slight wave in it, but always very elaborately styled, which framed her perfect, symmetrical face. Most people would say that the perfect nan does not exist, but Eloise disagreed, as she knew for a fact that her nan was perfect, her kindness and gentleness being just some of her amazing qualities. As Eloise felt the gentleness of her nan's hands, she stepped back and remembered as a child, how soft and delicate they were then, too. She smiled at Bea, who was looking rather elegant in her pink, flowered dress and matching bonnet. She had always possessed a unique style, quite simple yet always very elegant. 'Are you going somewhere?' 'Oh,' remarked Bea with a smile. 'I have just been for a leisurely walk and am making my way back to my home now. Would you care to join me?' Eloise had not seen her nan and grandads' home since she had arrived in heaven. 'Oh, that would be lovely,' she replied. 'I have a few things I need to be doing, so I will let you go with your nan,' Will piped up, as he bent over and dropped a gentle kiss lightly on Eloise's lips, a soft kiss on Bea's cheek, and within a moment, he was gone. As they continued to walk at a leisurely pace, a sweet scent filled the air as Eloise took in the beauty that enveloped her. 'Just look at this,' Bea said excitedly. Everywhere Eloise looked, a violet haze smothered the woodland floor like a cosmic river, as it filled the surrounding area with its aesthetic charm. 'Oh my,' she breathed at the wondrous sight all around. Bluebells were everywhere, bursting with delight as she stood in silence for a minute or two, captivated. 'Goodness! Exceptionally beautiful,' she gasped with wonder at the majestic landscape of blue carpeting that draped throughout the woodland, more and more inspired with every step that she took. Shards of dappled light cut through the canopied trees, as the sound of birds that flew overhead was a delight to hear as Eloise continued her walk amongst the bluebells that encircled her, as their strong, sweet scent continued to fill the air. A coating of white shingle glistened, making it easier to see ahead, as she took in all that surrounded her on either side of the track, whilst a huge oak tree stood up ahead of her, with its sturdy trunk and magnificent presence. Known as the king of the forest, for simply being the size that it was, stood proud with its large branches spread wide, whilst vibrant green leaves rustled gently in the breeze. Eloise continued just a little further, and it was not long before she had reached a walkway of steps, three in total, sat neatly nestled amongst a single spread of shingle. As she raised her foot to the first one, a light flashed on, and at that precise moment, she stopped in her tracks and turned to admire the beauty of what stood directly in front of her. A pure white building gleamed. 'Oh wow!' She cried, astounded by all that she could see. The light lit up every detail of what stood in front of Eloise's eyes. 'I never expected this!' The house sat amidst lush, vibrant flowers, giving out an aroma of charm and tranquillity, with the lawn looking like a fresh carpet had just been fitted. 'Nan, it's stunning.' 'Thank you, my dear,' replied Bea. 'This is Golden Horizon. Do let me show you some more.' Eloise's face lit up with delight, and she could not wait to see what her nan and grandad's house was like inside.

Roses, Lilies, and Sunflowers surrounded the front garden in an assortment of colours, making the complete garden look stunning, and Eloise knew then that the inside of the house was going to be so full of love. Just a few more steps and both she and her nan had reached the front gate. Bea led the way as Eloise eyed the surroundings of the whole front garden, as an oasis of shrubs and a narrow path of cobbled stone led the way towards the front entrance. As her nan opened what looked like a freshly painted door, a brightness beamed from the inside, and Eloise was flabbergasted by the open floor plan that stood in front of her, with its high ceilings. Everywhere was spacious, elegant, and beautiful with its light blue painted walls, and Eloise was astounded as she walked around the magnificent house, taking in all that filled the space before her. Velvet curtains hung from every tall, glass window, from which filled every room throughout, each one having a magnificent view and all letting in ample light. A huge piano stood in the corner of the main living area; its elegant, classical look stood proud, and although the piano used to be Beas's passion, she had not played it in a while. Just across the room, stood two large suites of a dark blue, placed either side of each other, whilst vases of freshly cut flowers, that filled every space throughout, gave out the most incredible fragrance. The rest of the furniture in the house gave great comfort and style, fitting in with all that Eloise's nan and grandad had always loved, and as Eloise herself wandered throughout the house, she could not help but feel a sense of awe at all the hard work that had been put into making such a construction of sheer beauty.

A fully fitted kitchen led just off the lounge with every top-of-the-range appliance you could possibly ever want or need, and a smell of warm cinnamon cakes wafted up from the oven as Eloise stepped into the magnificent room. 'It is all very beautiful here,' she stated enthusiastically. 'Such a stunning abode filled with warmth and charm makes this home such a cherished home.' Bea smiled at her granddaughter and thanked her kindly, her smile being that of great warmth. A cosy reading room could be seen just ahead, where several bookcases stood erect against the main wall, filled with hundreds of books of all kinds. Bea loved to read; she had always said that it allowed her to imagine herself in the story as if she was really living in that moment, and Eloise understood exactly what she meant by that, as it was the same feeling she got herself, every time she wrote a book!

As they headed back to the lounge, where huge glass sliding doors stood tall, Bea led the way out onto a marbled terrace, which was filled with an oasis of pots, as she stepped down onto a lawn of pure greenery. Trees laden with fruit, cherry, apple, and peach, stood all around, as hedges separated the other houses, and Eloise was taken aback once more as her eyes feasted on all the stunning colours of the flowers around her. Reds, pinks, oranges, and lilacs stood proud in delicate pastels as they let out a sweet scent. Beas garden was certainly a place of tranquillity and beauty, so Eloise thought, as she stood still for a second as a sense of peace washed over her. It was at that moment that she spotted her grandad at the bottom of the garden, lying on what looked like the most comfortable recliner she had ever seen, and once again, sleeping, and with his handkerchief on his head. She had a little smirk to herself as he continued to sleep like a baby, only snoring here and there, unaware of what was going on around him.

As swans and ducks passed by in the small river that ran through her nan's garden, Eloise stood admiring their gracefulness. 'Come and sit down for a while.' Bea tapped her hand on the nearby chair, inviting her granddaughter to join her as they began to chat about old times. 'Do you remember Nan?' she asked. 'The time when we went shopping with mum and you had odd shoes on?' 'Yes,' Bea chuckled. 'Only no one realised until we had got almost all the way to the shops, but then it was too late.' Eloise began laughing with her nan. Beas' laugh was always of a gentle but joyful sound. 'I also remember the day I had tea at yours and you cooked scrambled eggs and I hated it.' 'Oh yes,' said Bea. 'I remember that moment, you had an almighty tantrum because I told you that you had to eat it all and that you were not leaving the table until then.' It was how children were brought up back then, to be grateful for what food was put in front of them and to respect one another for what they were given, and Eloise knew not to disrespect her nan in any way. She had always had such an unconditional love for her nan, and growing up, she always remembered Beas' comforting words, always assuring her that all would be okay, no matter what.

Whilst catching up and giggling like a couple of school children, a voice startled her. Hendrix had woken from his nap, and as he welcomed her with open arms, his handkerchief had since been tucked inside the pocket of his jacket. 'Grandad, it is so good to see you.' Eloise gave him a very much-needed hug. 'I did see you when I was with Will,' she continued, looking up at him with a smile. 'You were at an allotment of some sort.' 'Oh yes, my dear, I have many crops growing there now. You must come and look at my potatoes, green beans, and carrots. I have a mixture of fruit too. Strawberries, blackberries, blueberries and much more. Eloise smiled once again at her grandad. 'I shall do that. I did call to you,' she said. 'Oh, you will never wake him,' piped up Bea. 'Well, not unless you have a gong bell to strike in his ear.' They all laughed as they continued to catch up with old times for a while longer.

After much gasbagging, Eloise felt she should make her way and let her grandparents get some rest, only they thought differently. Standing upright and still trying to take everything in, her grandad piped up, 'Come,' he beamed. 'Your nan and I have a little something to show you.' Both bright-eyed, with a spring in their step as if they were still a young

couple, they led the way. 'I am intrigued!' Cried
Eloise as she wandered out of the gate, her nan and
grandad slightly ahead. All through the grounds,
several people walked as children ran alongside some
of them, whilst other people sat amongst the trees and
shrubs, most likely taking in the beautiful
surroundings, Eloise thought. A cool breeze blew as
they walked along the stunning footpaths, passing a
variety of blossom trees that surrounded them on
either side. Just a short walk further, and they soon
came to the most beautiful grounds, and Eloise knew
immediately why her nan and grandad had brought
her here, for this was the exact thing that they both
loved. A sunburst of gold with scorching oranges and
molten reds stood out ahead, and Eloise could not
quite believe what she was seeing. It was like a lake
of pure colour, surrounded by the greenest of green
blades of grass. They stood silent for a moment, just
taking in all the glorious colour and scent of every
flower that lay in front of them. 'My, my!' Eloise
belted out. 'What a magnificent, stunning array of
flowers,' she added. 'There must be every colour that
is imaginable, standing right here, with the most
amazing scent that you could only ever dream of
smelling.' She could not believe that around every
corner she walked was another aromatic piece of
exquisite scenery, and she was looking forward to
what else lay ahead in this picturesque land. Both Bea
and Hendrix smiled in Eloise's direction, pleased that
she loved what she was seeing in front of her, as they

guided her further along. Countless shades of pink blossom bloomed, and Eloise was mesmerised by the beauty and the perfumed scent that rose from each tree. 'Do you know what the blossom represents?' Bea asked. 'No!' Eloise answered, shaking her head. 'Rebirth, and new beginnings. They are a symbol of love, affection, happiness, hope, and joy.' 'How do you know all this, Nan?' Eloise asked with a smile. 'I have learnt about all that is here in heaven, and you shall too,' Bea replied. 'If you look closely, you will see most of the trees have dark pink blossom, which is because they are in bud. When they first blossom, they turn to a lighter pink, and some are white.' Eloise was astounded by all that her nan knew, as she took in every word to remember for herself. Blossom Garden was a place that people in heaven quite often went to as they liked to enjoy a leisurely walk amongst the oasis of beautiful trees with their vibrant colours and lush greenery, not to mention capturing the essence of every blossom. 'This is where your grandad likes to spend most of his time,' said Bea. 'For there is so much beauty here, and nature, which he loves.' 'Will you look at that!' Piped up Hendrix, pointing. It was a tapestry of nature's wonder, as butterflies flew above their heads, gliding from left to right. Eloise could fully understand why her grandad loved coming here and felt grateful to be in such a serene and beautiful setting.

It was not long after taking in all the delightful colours that stood in front of her and all the nature, that Bea and Hendrix decided to let their granddaughter make her way. For now, they said their farewells and headed back to their beautiful house to rest.

Because Eloise had lived across the road from her grandparents growing up, she had the great privilege of always having the opportunity to visit them whenever she liked, and she was always grateful for that. They were such wonderful people, and Eloise knew why her mum was the way she was, always there to listen, always calm, so gentle, and with such a loving heart. There was no denying that the love Eloise had for her nan and grandad had always been strong, and seeing them again had brought joy to her heart and made her feelings for them even stronger. She had never told them just how much she had loved them before coming to heaven, or that their presence had always been a gentle spirit of kindness that always left a forever mark, which is why a large piece of them stayed with her in her heart after they both passed.

CHAPTER 18

Eloise woke to the warming rays of light as they filtered through her window in a scintillating cascade of colours, casting a radiant glow in the room, as she reflected on the time she had spent with God. A strong but soothing range of heavenly music suddenly washed over her at what sounded like at least a million voices, as they sang in worship of him. She was caught up in the heavenly tones as each one was captivating in their wondrous pitch. It was the most beautiful and pleasant sound she had ever heard, and she felt embraced by it, as songs were sung one after the other, each one coming together as melodious as the next and every word sung was coming from the heart. Rubbing her bleary eyes, she rose to her feet, whilst pulling back the blinds, and observed the glorious, tranquil setting in front of her, pausing for a minute, thinking about not just the nature that surrounded her, but the people, the beautiful settings of all that she had seen. The stunning views, the spectacular colours in every flower and the variety of sweet fragrances in every single one. Every moment that she was spending in this beautiful place made her appreciate exactly what heaven was, as she took in all its glory.

She headed off with Will into the undulating beauty that stretched before her eyes, hoping she would be able to cram in as much as possible, as dried leaves of copper brown crunched beneath her feet as she walked, whilst observing and taking in all that heaven had to offer.

Amidst the forest of crisp, fresh air, all was clear as she trudged along, taking in her daily dose of charm. Ranunculus flowers stood tall in their paper-thin spirals, amongst birds of paradise, with their fluttering wings and slender bodies, as all stood impressively in their vibrant colours. Eloise froze on the spot, amazed by all that she was seeing in front of her. 'They all provide such a haven of serenity, don't they?' She whispered as she breathed in the sweet, infused aroma that the flowers were giving off. 'Isn't nature wonderful?' She smiled, and with a heartwarming smile in return, Will continued to lead the way, allowing his love to enjoy the peacefulness and pureness that she remained holding on to. 'Where are we actually going?' Eloise felt as though she was always asking this question. Although a simple one, really, she had thought, but from her perspective, where else was there to possibly go in this land of glory? 'We are almost there,' answered Will as they continued to hike along the trail that wound its way through the forest, until finally, they had reached the awaiting surprise that Will had longed to show his love. Just at that moment, Eloise stumbled as she lost her footing. 'Easy now,' said Will as he caught a sudden grip of her hand. 'Are you okay?' She straightened herself, flexing her leg to check no damage had been done. 'Yes, a slight carelessness on my behalf.' A piece of wood lay over an empty brook of some sort, must have dried up, she thought! Will continued to lead the way, still holding tightly to Eloise's hand as he helped her across the plank. She was still none the wiser as to why he had brought her here. 'This'…... He paused for a second. 'Where we are standing right now, this is a valley, and behind this,' he pointed at all the trailing flowers that intertwined within one another. 'This is Paradise Garden, behind here,' he continued, pointing at what seemed to be nothing but a few flowers, and most of those were fully overgrown, spreading like wild flowers in fact. 'But there is nothing here,' Eloise cried. 'Oh, but there is,' he answered, as he began pulling the climbing flowers to one side. 'Like a secret garden! You mean to say, it is nestled behind all this?' She asked, as she gently pulled at the fragrant, trailing sweet pea in its ravishing mixture of colours, being careful not to break any. A solid piece of wood stood, buried in fact, as Eloise continued to help untangle more and more pieces, until a huge arched wooden gate, featuring a beautiful and eye-catching design, appeared before her. She stood back in amazement, her mouth wide open. 'Go on,' spoke Will. 'Open it.' Eloise felt for the latch, and with a gentle push, the gate slowly opened.

A golden path shimmered in the light, and at that moment, a warm feeling filled her inside, creating a sense of mystery at what lay beyond. Upon entering, she was welcomed by a magnificent aroma, and it was as if she had been transported into a whole new world, as she felt a sense of awe and wonder! Wildflowers lined the edges of the golden path, their vibrant colours standing out like a Loriini in a tree. Bees buzzed from flower to flower as butterflies flitted their delicate wings as they glided through the air, in and out of the branches of the trees, whilst Apples, plums, and pears stood as proud as they would in an orchard. The pathway was surrounded by an archway of trellising. Trails, and trails of it, with colours and colours of Clematis, Sweet Pea and climbing rose, covering every bit, and as fifty or more, wide, deep steps led the way down, Eloise could only describe it as exquisite. Taking Will's hand, she clutched it tightly, being careful not to fall again, as she took a step at a time down the cobblestone steps.

The garden was an oasis, and it was as if it told a story, a story of wonder and beauty, with hundreds of different trees, mainly evergreen ones. Panicles of scented, white flowers stood tall, as Juniper, with their green needle-like leaves and broad silver bands, curved slightly to a point. 'Once pollinated, remarked Will, 'they develop into purple, berry-like cones.' 'Are they edible?' Eloise asked. 'Yes, they are, although it is mostly birds that eat them. Would you like to try some?' Will picked a few off the tree and held them out in his hand. 'I think I will pass on that,' was Eloise's response, her nose scrunched up. 'The fresh Juniper is juicy, whereas the dried berries have a more citrus flavour with a piney spiciness to them.'

'Not really my thing,' added Eloise. Will laughed at her comment as they both continued to walk on. Magnolia Grandiflora trees stood proud, with their large, glossy, leathery leaves and large white flowers, letting out the most beautiful scent as Will and Eloise passed them by. 'You would find it difficult to find a flower as large and beautiful as this one in a garden on earth,' announced Will, pointing at the cup-shaped flowers on the tree. As he continued to show his love around the stunning gardens, Eloise recognised that each path had a curve, creating a curiosity within her as to what was coming next. Hundreds, thousands of flowers, mainly lavender and lilies, delighted her senses with both their aroma and colours. Honeysuckle, clematis, and wisteria captured her imagination as they twisted in and out of the trellising that ran along the back of this exquisite place she was standing in. Wind chimes, beautifully crafted, added a touch of elegance in the garden as they filled the air with their enchanting, soothing tunes, creating an oasis of tranquillity. Under another arch and along another path going off in yet a different direction, where stems of more climbing flowers covered the walls of the paradise garden, whilst grasses rustled around the apple and plum trees that were lined up like soldiers on parade. 'What are these?' Eloise picked up a small rock with the word 'love' on it. She had noticed there were several darted about as she walked around, and all had different words on them. 'They are kindness rocks, well'...... went on Will.

'They are pebbles/stones that people here have painted and decorated either with a picture or a word to inspire creativity here, but also to make those who find them feel even more happiness than they already do.' 'That is so lovely,' replied Eloise, smiling. 'Yes. It is said that once someone has found one, they can hand it to whoever they wish to for a short while, then that person puts it back somewhere in the garden. But only in this garden.' 'Oh, what a beautiful thing to do,' Eloise smiled once more. It gave her an idea of something she would love to do with the children.

Beautiful arched trellising continued to stand proud, as Roses, lilacs, and lobelia trailed in and out, over, and around with their stunning cascade of colour, as birds flew over Eloise's head, chirping to one another. As a wide cobbled stone path trailed in and out, interweaving amongst shelters of trees, she was excited as to where it was to lead to, as she observed all that heaven had to offer in this beautiful garden. Just ahead, in the middle of a courtyard, a fountain stood. A black stone fountain, and whilst its sparkling, clear water ran freely, a robin stood with its feet in the water, as it gently paddled, whilst two robins sat perched on the edge, minding their own business. Eloise drew close, but the birds did not fly away; in fact, they let her stroke them as they let out their soft chirps.

Although the garden was filled with a heady perfume of blooming scents, so intoxicating that it seemed to caress Eloise wherever she stood, it filled her with a deep sense of peace and contentment, and it was at that moment that both she and Will decided what better place to take a short rest and take in all the beauty that surrounded them. A table and chairs of white wrought iron were tucked away amongst the flowers across from the bird bath, as two giant flowerpots stood at either side of the table, with petunias, adding a burst of vibrant hues, whilst canna lilies stood extravagantly in their gorgeous shades of orange and red. A vast amount of people could be spotted amongst the secluded areas of seating, each one likely to be enjoying and taking in the glorious surroundings of the beautiful garden, so Eloise suspected. 'This is especially popular for couples to come to,' said Will. 'It really is one of the most peaceful of places here in heaven.' 'It really is a garden of paradise,' replied Eloise, 'like its name says,' she added, and just as a gentle trickling of water flowed from the edge of the stone fountain, a soothing, melodious sound of wind chimes was heard, whilst a gentle breeze blew and filled the garden with calming music. Every aspect of the garden was a delight to behold, which left Eloise with an incredible mark on her soul. All that she had seen gave her a deep sense of contentment, leaving her feeling even more connected to beautiful heaven.

It had been yet another outstanding day of not just seeing all that was around her in this delightful place of purity, but learning so much that fulfilled every part of her being, to which she had never expected.

CHAPTER 19

Unaware that she had nodded off, Eloise was quite refreshed after a full rest and doze and could not help but feel grateful to be starting another day in such a serene and tranquil place as she embarked on what lay ahead.

A bright, beautiful light flashed before her as she followed Will outside, taking in the beautiful smells that filled the air whilst observing all that nature had to offer. The walk with him offered even more truly astounding views, as the enchanting scents around her drew her in. Shades of pink, purple and red were a symphony of colour as they stood in an array at every pace she took, creating an atmosphere of pure serenity. 'Here, I found these for you, my love.' Eloise stopped in her tracks as Will handed her a couple of sweet-scented freesias. 'Oh, my goodness! They are beautiful,' she said, sniffing the aroma coming from the beautiful array. 'Thank you so much.' Will's arms gently hugged her, and as he gave her a gentle kiss on the cheek, a bright glow filled Eloise's face as she continued walking at a slow pace, one hand holding her flowers whilst the other was in Will's, and as he looked at her, he gave a sultry smile. 'Where are we going?' She questioned, not recognising the path she was walking on! 'Nestled deep within the heart of heaven,' he added. 'Lies a hidden beauty.' 'Oh, what more could there possibly be in this magnificent land?' replied Eloise, waiting eagerly as to what was going to come next! 'A hidden beauty of what?' She waited for his answer. 'A surprise within an opening.' Mmmmmm!' She added, intrigued. 'That all sounds mysterious.' 'Oh, but wait until you see what is inside,' Will replied. 'This is entirely different from anything you have seen since you have been here.' 'You're not giving much away, are you?' Eloise smiled as she continued to ramble through this beautiful land, appreciating its surroundings, as a crispness crackled with each step she took. There were several people walking to and fro, none that she recognised, but all said hello with a warm and friendly smile, so she smiled back, eager now to reach the surprise, as she covered trails and trails of narrow pathways, whilst appreciating the scenery, noticing the bright yellow and white flowers that bloomed along the trail. She eventually reached an opening in a rock. 'This is The Whispering Sanctuary.' Will pointed at the hole that was formed within the rock face and surrounded by a variety of natural greenery. 'Crikey!' Remarked Eloise, her mouth wide open as she could just about make out the tiny entrance in front of her. 'You can kind of understand where they get the name 'keyhole,' for a passage/opening,' she stated, as she just stood and stared at the small gap, in fact, it was so small that she would never have known it was there if Will had not said so! Anxiety rushed over her body at the thought of entering the terrain, and she hesitated for a bit, worried if she would be able to face her fear and overcome this obstacle, as an uneasiness filled her body at the thought of being in a confined space, but she knew the only way to deal with another one of her fears was to face it head on. The entrance was ready to welcome her, and although she was quite short, she still felt she had to stoop a little to enter without bumping her head.

She half expected a dark and dreary entrance and a colony of bats welcoming her, flying over her head, forcing her to take Will's hand in a tight grip, but instead, she was immediately struck with wonder, as a feeling of delight suddenly filled her insides. The more steps she took, the more the inside unfolded like a hidden world. 'It is beautiful,' she stated, as she stood still for a moment, taking in all that was around her. It was not dark at all, as small lights twinkled, coming from the crystalline stalactites that hung like chandeliers, and as she walked on slowly, each step echoed throughout as pathways of crumbled shingle led to an opening, which seemed like a mysterious tunnel. Eloise noticed how the walls of this angelic opening shone, like diamonds sparkling within a kaleidoscope, as each light filled her with awe and hope, knowing that the Lord was guiding her. Each rock ranged from bright orange to deep red, giving out a breathtaking beauty of wonder, whilst little alcoves shimmered drops of water within the rock formations on the walls, each image being of God on his throne, he that ruled heaven, in an absorbing tapestry of love.

The visual surroundings were beautiful and serene as Eloise encountered some concrete steps, the complete flight, supported by a bannister of glass. It was something she had never seen before or even ever imagined could ever be, as the glass shone clear, giving out a form of elegance and sophistication. Looking down at the steep drop, she was aware that there were three levels, each with its own glass panelling, which took her breath away. Lost for words at the exquisite surroundings that stood before her, grateful that it allowed her and each person that entered it to admire the beauty, but moreover, letting in an enchanting flow of natural light. She took one step at a time whilst scurrying to, eager to reach the bottom, but Will stopped her in her tracks as she had reached the first level. 'Oh my!' Was all she could manage, as she took in the gloriousness of the pool that shone before her. The shimmering of the water was mesmerising as it enveloped her with warmth, soothing her eyes and refreshing her mind as Will continued to lead her down to the next level. Another pool stood in all its glory, with the same blueness sparkling like a cluster of diamonds in a ring, undisturbed, not a ripple of movement, and as she ventured deeper, the sanctuary began to reveal all that was hidden. Not just the pools, but spaces for worshipping and reflecting and personal spaces for praying and focusing on God's presence and goodness. It was not just the grandeur of it that captivated Eloise, but also the silence all around.

She barely had a second to take in all its beauty as Will led her down the final stairway to see the last pool, and although it felt like it was taking a while, her hand began to get sweaty from the tight grip she had on the glass hand rail and the thoughts that filled her head were concerning her a little as she was beginning to feel a little claustrophobic. She took a slow breath before entering deeper into the sanctuary, so as not to go into a massive meltdown, whilst Will kept a tight grip of her other hand. As they explored further, she was able to breathe a sigh of relief once she had reached the bottom. 'Wow!' She cried, as she looked up, realising just how far down she had walked, overwhelmed with wonder as to the gloriousness that filled this beautiful sanctuary. Stopping in her tracks, she just glared, taking in every detail that stood before her in this stunning crystal wonderland. Welcomed by the glorious sight of the third crystal-clear pool, golden slabs filled every space, and Eloise was immediately enveloped within a sense of awe, as the pools within the sanctuary gave a magical glow throughout, whilst the gentle sound of dripping water echoed all around, adding a sense of tranquillity. 'What a spellbinding place this is,' she remarked, as she proceeded towards the pool, 'and so peaceful to,' she added. Will glanced across at her with a smile, 'It is simply breathtaking, yes.' 'It is the most beautiful and impressive place I have ever seen,' she replied, as she ventured around the sanctuary, the blue water shining as the magnificent rock formations shimmered like a captivating wonderland. Barely a sound was heard, all but a trickling of water from the pool, as sprays tickled her face. 'People come here often,' Will spoke out. 'Sometimes just to sit, but other times to pray.' 'I guess today is my day,' Eloise added. 'How lucky am I?' She piped up, grateful, being able to see this all for herself. 'I am intrigued, though, as to why it is called 'The Whispering Sanctuary?' 'Well, it is said that divine whispers of guidance can be heard here, from the rocks, but it is said that it is God guiding us,' he answered. Eloise certainly felt the connection, and it was at that moment that she felt a chill run through her body.

The sight and the smells, and just being in the sanctuary, were so mind-blowing, so peaceful that Eloise could not believe she was in heaven; it was as though she had just stepped into another world. Even the air that she breathed was fresh, and she could not believe that what she was witnessing was such beauty, and that it even existed. The highlight of the pools, so Eloise thought, was that of their design, and she could quite imagine herself having the chance to experience the most amazing sensation of just floating in one of them whilst taking in the most serene surroundings.

After spending a fair amount of time in this exquisite place and taking in all the unexpected glory that enveloped her, once back outside, the picturesque views surrounding the sanctuary grabbed Eloise's attention, even though it was just a quick glance. Beautiful, serene, and as peaceful as a quiet valley, the idyllic scene took her breath away and with a sigh, she left, sure to return to this hidden gem.

CHAPTER 20

Whilst Will went on his way, having a prior engagement to get to, Eloise chose this moment to explore heaven by herself, reflecting on all that she had seen so far and appreciating all its beauty. Apart from reuniting with loved ones, heaven was about the happiness and tranquillity that it fulfilled everyone with, and it was certainly doing that for Eloise. The nature of this beautiful place was to worship God, accept him, and the peace and joy he gave out to one and all, but it was also performing duties and tasks, helping one another, and it was something everyone loved to do; they were dedicated and passionate, and Eloise loved seeing everyone being there for one another. It was what they called 'A labour of love.' Selfless, motivated, and devoted, and she believed that this was the place where so many people, once they arrived here, would learn so, so much.

Shards of dappled light cut through the canopy of trees as Eloise continued forward with a leisurely stroll, breathing in every bit of glorious air that hung around her. Every walk she had here in heaven provided such a pure serenity, surrounded with natural beauty, scents, and sounds, which she loved, and it really could not get any better than all that she had seen so far! Sunflowers stood tall, their golden faces smiling in the gentle breeze, whilst the fresh air let out a sweet perfume of Lavender as squirrels playfully chased one another, darting up and down the trees with incredible spryness. Whilst on her walk, she was drawn to an expanse of greenery that stretched before her eyes, where an array of more beautiful flowers stood, arranged in a visually appealing manner. Just as she inhaled deeply, taking in the aroma of the petals from a yellow rose, it tickled her nose, and it was at that moment that she found herself submerged in peace and taken aback by what was on the grounds where she stood right now. Nestled amidst the tranquil beauty that stood before her, a serene and beautiful building stood. It was like nothing Eloise had seen since arriving in heaven. This enormous dome-shaped structure with four levels of solid concrete and more than forty steps that lead up to its entrance, was stretched out in front of her. Its huge pillars on either side, and stunning glass-stained windows, sparkled in the brightness, whilst the garden around it was filled with a blend of tranquillity, elegance, and natural beauty, as lanterns shone within the ferns, evergreens, and maples. This was a Temple. A beautiful Temple at that, and as Eloise mounted the steps, she noticed the beautiful sign on the door, 'We Welcome Everyone,' and thought it was a pleasant gesture.

Upon entering the building, although it was extremely spacious, she evoked a range of feelings, because the atmosphere within was peaceful and positive, including calm. The inner walls were covered with many paintings, those of God himself, and Eloise felt comfortable, a feeling of awe and a sense of belonging.

A figure of light shone, as a voice whispered, 'Come closer,' and Eloise knew it was God, for she felt peace, joy, love, and awe within her soul whilst remaining steadfast, as she tried to find the right words to say! 'Be open to him,' she told herself. 'But more importantly, be honest.' Not knowing what God's reaction was going to be, she just said it how it was, as she bowed her head before him. 'I apologise for what I did,' she voiced, quietly. 'For ending my life the way I did.' She hesitated for a moment. 'I.... I know it was a sin, but I also know that I am feeling so guilty, considering what others have been through, those who have had no choice but to die. Those that fought to the very end, but could no longer hold on!' She held back for a moment. 'I am so, so sorry,' she spoke out. 'I.... I....'She hesitated again, trying to find the right words, but it was at that moment that God spoke back in his gentle, soothing voice, telling Eloise that she was forgiven already, for she had repented, and he understood why she felt she had to do what she did. But that was not the reason why he had brought her to heaven, and Eloise was confused! 'I have brought you here, my child, because I want you to learn about yourself. You do not seem to realise how much you help others, but you never help yourself.' He went on. 'Eloise, you are a kind and caring person, you have a gift for bringing such love to so many people, a gift for helping all those around you, in so many ways, but….' He added. 'You must be able to think of yourself, for you need to be able to cope with your anxiety, depression, sadness, fears, amongst others, and all that has been breaking you.' Eloise just stood in awe. 'First,' said God. 'You must learn to love yourself, not just others, and secondly,' he added. 'Challenge any negative thoughts you have into making them positive ones, Eloise, and incorporate healthy thoughts. It is a must.' 'Yes,' she replied. It all started to make sense, like all the things that had been happening since her arrival, things that were not obvious to her, were in fact tests! God was the one who was encouraging her to take the lessons which he was giving her and guiding her. 'Yes…Yes, I will.' Eloise promised. 'I have begun to recognise and challenge my negative thoughts and fears, preparing myself mentally.' There was a silence for a short while, then…. 'Keep positive, and keep connecting yourself with all the people, like you have done since you came here,' added God. 'And remember, engage in prayer and reflection, ask me anytime for understanding and guidance.'

Eloise realised that being in heaven and being in the presence of God was teaching her so much, as well as freeing her from all her sorrow, suffering, and pain and was now filling her with peace, joy, and happiness. The emptiness she once felt submerging her inner body was now overflowing with safety, love, and acceptance, like all the pressure that she had been holding before had been lifted. 'I will continue to guide you and provide you with strength, but you must make your own choices. Find yourself, Eloise, and be that person. Keep positive, that is the key. If you put your mind to it, you, my child, can accomplish anything.' 'Yes… yes…. It all makes sense now,' she paused, and feeling uplifted, as she stood in this beautiful Temple with the Glory of God. 'I will do as you have asked,' she answered, before adding…. 'God, may… May I ask you something,' she hesitated for a moment. 'Go ahead, my child.' 'My stepfather, Duke, he was in his final days just before I arrived here, and I have prayed that you will let him go without suffering. I pray that you let him fall asleep and guide him home here, gently. Please let him go peacefully.'

Eloise felt a little numb inside as she remembered how Duke had become, and knew that as soon as his time was up, not only would he be arriving in this beautiful land, but he would also become the man he once was. No more suffering. No more pain…. He will be truly at rest.

Duke had been Eloise's second stepfather, following on from Eli, but she loved them both the same. Although they were quite different in their own way, they had the same qualities in being so caring. 'My child,' God whispered gently. 'I will tell you now, your stepfather, Duke, is here; only recently did he arrive, but I can assure you he is here; you must go see for yourself,' he added. 'You will find him at the marina.' Eloise bowed her head with a smile, feeling uplifted, and no sooner had the light of God appeared than it slowly dimmed, but she knew that he was always all around her, and as she left the Temple, she was content at what she had witnessed and felt a warm glow fill her body as she went on her way.

Eloise came to realise that she had never done so much walking as that, since her arrival in heaven, but here, it was so different. Here, it was more refreshing, and she felt a lot more connected with nature, enjoying all the sounds and sights. Here, she was fulfilled by scenes of beautiful colours, magnificent buildings adorned with every detail you could possibly dream of, stunning gardens, blooming with every coloured flower you ever thought existed, and trees bearing every fruit you could ever want. Waterfalls and lakes. Who thought they would even exist in heaven! As she continued her walk through pretty lanes, where many of the winding paths intersected with picturesque flower beds, she observed and took in all that was around her, as her mind went back to Duke.

Standing at over six feet, with white wispy hair and thinning out in more places than others, he was a gentle giant with a cheeky grin upon his face, because he was always so cheerful. He lived for the moment and reminded everyone to always laugh, for laughing was the medicine to a happy life. So, he believed! He always kept his cards close to his chest and kept himself to himself most of the time, although he was, however, very close to his stepdaughters and their partners. Deni (Eloise's mum) and Duke's wife had always been Duke's rock, and he would do anything for her, even if it meant travelling to the other side of the world and back for her! He always looked after Deni, but the roles reversed when he became ill, and it was not long before the dementia took over his life, quicker than anyone had ever believed it would. Eloise imagined that her mum must be feeling distraught right now, after losing her beloved husband, leaving her with a rollercoaster of emotions, a tapestry of pain and an overwhelming feeling of emptiness. There was also the profound sorrow for the loss of the man she once knew and the relationship they once had before his dementia. But Eloise believed that her mum would be relieved in a way, knowing that Duke would no longer be suffering in the lost world of his brain and was now at peace. Now in heaven, where he would be very much at rest.

As Eloise walked through the heavenly grounds, covering tracks she had not passed through before, she came up against even more grandeur as she immersed herself within the tranquillity of nature that was all around her, as it provided and invigorated a calming atmosphere. Each path was lined with vibrant green as wildflowers swayed gently, whilst beauty filled the area. The marina was not far, and somehow Eloise managed to keep on track as to where she was going, as these magnificent paths set in the heart of heaven led her to a vast open space just up ahead. The trees seemed to thin out as a shimmering expanse of water came into a truly unique view, where a selection of houseboats stood. The beauty was unbelievable and certainly something to admire, Eloise thought. An exclusive and elegant place that filled her with warmth.

Each of the houseboats were nestled amongst the shoreline of the 'Blue Horizon Marina,' it being a tranquil and secluded setting. They were basically a house on water, and Eloise was not surprised at all at her stepfather having one of these, as he always loved the water. A 45ft houseboat with its unique blend of elegance stood in this beautiful setting where Eloise was right now. The base (hull), being the body of the boat, the structure that provided the main support, stood solid, with the house itself sitting firmly on top. It looked stunning, so Eloise thought, as it incorporated plenty of charm, and with the timeless and versatile cream in which it was painted, it brought out a subtle warmth and contentment to the whole thing. It was as she drew closer that she spotted her stepfather sitting on the veranda, cross-legged, although looking rather relaxed. He seemed to be quite protected by a large retractable canopy, which Eloise presumed was providing the necessary shade in which he needed, whilst papers lay on a small table beside him, some neatly stacked, whilst others lay scattered. 'Duke,' she called in a gentle voice so as not to startle him. 'Duke,' she called again, and as he turned to face Eloise, his once sad and lost smile had returned to a glowing and happy grin. 'Eloise! Eloise!' He beamed as he rose from his seat to face her. 'What a joy it is to see you again. Come, come aboard, but mind the gangway as you go,' he added. 'I have not quite fathomed the best form of a step yet.' Is a gangway not what you get on a cruise ship! Eloise thought. Maybe he looked upon this as his 'ship,' bless him. Even so, she smiled as she carefully walked the plank, almost falling into Duke's arms. 'Oh! Oh!' She cried. 'Mind how you go now,' Duke said, as he grabbed his stepdaughter's arm, saving her from falling flat on her face.

Regardless of what just happened, the image of her stepfather looking not only relaxed but also extremely well was a powerful and touching image. 'It is so lovely to see you,' she said as they embraced. His appearance was that of how he once looked before his dementia, not just his face, but his overall presentation, and Eloise could see that he was lifted by this. 'Well!' She piped up. 'I am loving this here, this is definitely you, Duke,' she smiled, gazing at the deck, a perfect place to sit and admire the waterfront environment and all its wildlife, and enjoying all the peaceful sounds of the water. 'Well, yes, you know how much I love boats and water, so I thought, why not have a houseboat on the water, combine the two,' he added. Eloise loved the logic in his thinking! 'Come, take a look around,' he said joyously. 'Oh! I hope I was not interrupting anything?' 'No…No.' Duke replied. 'I was just doing a bit of writing.' Eloise gave a perceptible smile, for she recalled the time Duke had begun writing a book many moons ago, although, sadly, never completed it. 'You know me,' he went on. 'Always starting something, but never finishing it.' 'But.' Eloise added. 'You may never have finished things for yourself, but you were always helping others, and everyone always appreciated that.' She paused, waiting for a response, but nothing. Instead, as Duke tidied his papers into a reasonably neat pile, she called his name, trying to gain his attention. 'Duke!' She hesitated for a moment, but still nothing! So, she tried another tactic. 'You know something?' She asked. But once again, nothing! 'I do not think I have ever said thank you to you for all the times you helped me out, I have never really told you how much I appreciated all that you did for me.' Duke just stood and smiled. He was never one for really showing emotion or acting on it, but Eloise thought he might have said something! 'Let me show you around,' he added sharpish, changing the subject, so Eloise just smiled and let it go. Duke was a good man, an incredible man, and seeing him here in heaven as his old self made Eloise smile. Seeing him on this magnificent houseboat also made her smile, and as she walked around it, she believed it to be everything that her stepfather loved.

She felt the interior offered a unique blend of personalised décor and basic living, just how Duke liked. 'Oh yes, this is your style,' she remarked, looking at the cosy, rustic space in front of her. 'Plenty of storage space, I see,' she added. 'Always handy, and I am loving the large windows letting in the beauty of the light. What a stunning place you have here.' She just stood quietly for a moment, looking at the luxurious dwelling as she gazed around at the beauty that she was standing on, as well as the picturesque views that stood before her. Duke's houseboat sat in its own personal corner of this paradise, and for him, it was a whole new world, a perfect balance, providing him with a space of wellbeing and a great sense of fulfilment. Eloise turned to her stepfather for a moment, as she thought about what she had done, what brought her to Heaven, believing she owed him an explanation. 'I am sorry, Duke, for what I have done, for purposely ending my life when you were fighting so hard to keep living yours.' 'Hey, hang on a minute,' replied Duke. 'Do not ever be sorry, for you had your reasons for what you did, and even though I might not understand why, I shall not judge you for your actions.' He went on. 'And yes, I may have kept fighting to begin with, but I chose to stop in the end, not just for myself, but for your mum.' Eloise fought to hold back the emotion she was feeling inside at this precise moment. 'I did not want your mum to sit by my bed day in, day out, watching me deteriorate, minute by minute, neither was it any life for me,' he added. Eloise knew her stepfather was right. What life was it for him? What life was it for her mother to live daily? Even though there would always be the profound sorrow, Deni would be relieved that Duke was in a better place now.

'I am just relieved that you are no longer suffering,' said Eloise, 'but are instead here, in this beautiful place. She smiled as she gave her stepfather a gentle hug. 'Mind how you go now,' said Duke, as he gave her a helping hand. Eloise was careful this time, making sure to avoid tripping up again. 'I will see you soon, he added.' She had only taken a few steps when she stopped in her tracks and turned to face Duke once more. 'Did you forget something?' He called out. 'Yes…. Yes, I want to say thank you, Duke,' she replied, now facing him. 'Thank you for being a great stepfather to me, for treating me as your own, and I want you to know that I will always be thankful to you for being the man that came into my mum's life, for filling her life with love, and caring about her the way you did.' As Eloise hugged her stepfather once again, it suddenly occurred to her that in all the time that Duke was alive, she had never once told him that she had loved him! Had she taken it for granted that he just knew! Perhaps now was the moment to tell him, she thought! Just keep it simple! 'Duke,' she whispered into his ear. 'I love you.' She hugged him once again before walking away, and as she glanced back over her right shoulder, she smiled, and in return, he called out, 'I love you too, Eloise.'

CHAPTER 21

Cradling her pillow, Eloise had slept peacefully after her previous moment with Duke, as rays of light filtered through the open window, which caused her to stir. Slowly, her mind woke from the stillness of all that was around her, as thoughts filled her head as to what might lie ahead for yet another perfect day. Breathing in the crisp morning air, she rose to see Will standing by the bedside, smiling. 'Are you ready for another exciting day, my love?' He asked, as he took her by the hand and kissed the back of it gently. 'Oh, most definitely,' she replied, a warm glow to her soft cheeks.

A bright, beautiful light flashed in front of Eloise as she left the house, the heat hitting the back of her neck as she walked. She could not believe there were so many paths, yet all looking so different, as Will led her in a new direction. Her eyes did not know where to look first, but astounded by this one, like all the others, it was a scene of pure perfection. A strong aroma of flowers wafted up as she waded in and out amongst the trees, grateful for those that shaded her from the heat. A variety of birds flew in and out amongst the branches, mostly Doves, with their small heads and stubby legs, and Eloise knew they would not harm her, for she had been told that all of God's creatures here in heaven were gentle and calm. The Blue Jays, with their striking blue feathers and black and white markings, jeered as they flew overhead; apparently, the sound helps them keep track of other Jays. Eloise proceeded ahead until she came to a large river that curved gently throughout a canopy of coconut trees. Known as trees of life in heaven, with their slim, smooth trunks, and being one of the most versatile in this beautiful land. The atmosphere was tranquil and bright as crystals as they stopped in their tracks. 'This is the River of Life,' piped up Will. 'Oh, isn't this the river that represents a never-ending flow of God's grace?' Eloise asked. 'Yes, well done for remembering that!' Will was quite astounded, but pleased that his fiancée was getting to grip with all that she was learning! 'It brings life to everyone as a source of nourishment, healing, and blessing,' he added. 'The deeper you form a relationship with God, the more the river of life will surround you and flow through you. It will bring a blessing to you, whenever it passes,' he smiled. Eloise was so grateful to all that she kept learning in this heavenly place, even if she could not hold every bit of information in her head.

As they continued to walk on, it was not long before they had reached a turn-off point, where a pathway of just a single line of paving slabs lay, and an assortment of flowers stood, each one perfectly placed. Eloise was immediately struck by the vibrant colours that surrounded her, each one letting out a sweet, infused aroma, whilst shimmering rays tickled each petal as they swirled in the gentle breeze. She was immediately enthralled, being exactly as Will had described, as the warmth continued to beam through the trees, and the air still smelled of every beautiful flower that bloomed, following them in every direction they bounced. She talked joyously with Will as they walked at a leisurely pace in this stunning land, his hand holding hers gently, as the two of them, content as one and other, happily proceeded to their next enchanting place.

Children were playing up ahead, and some were sitting with an elderly lady, as she told stories to them. Grownups walked hand in hand, others sat on benches chatting, and as Will and Eloise continued their walk, taking a variety of paths, leaves brushed up against them as those on the ground rustled beneath their feet. All Eloise could hear in the forest was the sound of nature, as birds sang their melodious tunes, squirrels scurried, rabbits scuttered, whilst all around her, blooming flowers stood. She was in awe of the sheer beauty that surrounded her and could not believe just how many different sections there seemed to be in heaven, and even though it was all one place, there were so many different directions you could possibly go. It was a glorious sight to see, and Eloise was captivated by the surroundings, which made her feel totally at peace in this land of paradise, for it was another piece of wonder that God had given her and all those amongst her. She was grateful for all that she had learnt too, since being in beautiful heaven and surprised that she had gained so much knowledge, but being in this amazing place was where she had longed to be for so, so long, for her life here was perfect.

A blissful brook sat ahead, its crystal-clear water shimmered like little white particles, and all around was brightly coloured sweet alyssum, with their small and dainty blossoms, with clusters of tiny pink, white, and purple flowers that only nature here could be responsible for. A weeping waterfall cascaded from a small gap in one of the rocks that stood proudly like a fragment of glass, as it sparkled behind the brook. 'I cannot believe what my eyes are seeing,' uttered Eloise as she faced Will. 'This place is quite stunning.' 'Oh. It really is unquestionably,' piped up Will with a huge smile upon his face. Eloise's gaze returned to the weeping waterfall, with its frothy cascade, as it plunged into the brook below. The brook itself travelled throughout the forest, gradually thinning out to a sand bank filled with pebbles, and as Eloise continued her way, it was not long before she had reached a winding path of an assortment of stones, as hues of purple, silver, red and blue and of vitreous appearance, stretched in front of her. The pure beauty of every stone that sparkled reflected its true essence within the surroundings she walked, carpeting every step that she made. 'Such a mixture,' she stated joyously. 'Which one is your favourite?' Questioned Will. 'I do not really have a favourite.' 'I bet you did not know that every individual stone has a unique meaning too,' Will teased her. 'N…... No, I did not.' 'Well,' he added. 'Some are a symbol of purity, others, of hope, calmness, peace, and sincerity.' Eloise smiled. 'I love them all, because they all have such warm tones and a delicateness about them, everyone adding a touch of elegance.' Will returned her smile.

It was just a few steps more when Eloise caught a glimpse of a wooden building, an immense one at that! All around stood the most beautiful of flowers, as bursts of colour and fragrances came from each one of them, with their pink and yellow petals blooming. Delicate pastels to vibrant shades filled the space around her, whilst each one gave a calming and peaceful feel to the building, and as vines and flowers grew up and over the glass-fitted windows, they glistened from the light that shone through. Eloise stopped in her tracks as she watched the butterflies, as they flitted from tree to tree, their delicate wings shimmering in the light, whilst birds sang their soothing tunes as they flew from branch to branch. 'Isn't nature beautiful?' she said to Will. 'So calming,' she added, feeling totally connected to all that she continued to see in this wonderland. 'Come,' insisted Will, smiling as he extended his hand, taking Eloise's in his. As he opened the tall oak door, trimmed in golden, Eloise immediately noticed the aroma that filled the air, whilst blends of freshly cooked food filled the building. A glamorous chandelier hung from the ceiling, lighting up the pink pastel walls that stood all around them. 'Brace yourself now, my love,' whispered Will, squeezing

Eloise's hand gently, and as he pushed the heavy door with his other hand, a warm and welcoming atmosphere filled the room and space around her as she entered. Every single person that she had met up with, since arriving in heaven, plus those that she had not seen yet, filled the room as they stood tall with smiles upon their faces. Her nans and grandads, her mother and father-in-law, her stepdads, aunties and uncles, cousins, friends, and others that she recognised that had passed way back, and of course, her father. She was truly grateful to be surrounded by so many and in such a glorious place. Eloise fought to hold back her tears. Tears of joy, of course! 'Oh, how wonderful is this,' she stood still for a moment, lost in thought, as she looked around the room at all those who filled the space. 'Are you okay, my love?' Said Will as he gave her a consoling pat on the back. 'Yes, just a little overwhelmed,' she replied, looking at all the people who stood before her.

Whilst everyone began to mingle, having great conversations, Eloise could not help but eye up all that filled the room in its exquisite form of luxury. Each wall, a subtle lemon, with its most monumental of chandeliers, hung from the ceiling, but it was the long oval table that drew her attention. Made of deep oak and a thick layer of marble, as it stood proudly in the centre of the room. Beautifully laid, with fresh flowers at each end and elegant tableware, it created an inviting ambience, whilst the soft lighting gave a gentle glow over the plush seating, leaving Eloise astounded.

Being the perfect gentleman, Will pulled out a chair for her to sit, as the conversation that was had by all, suddenly went from a constant chitter chatter, to complete silence as all the guests' eyes were now on the butler. A butler! Eloise had thought. In heaven! But even so, he stood tall and proud, in his black suit, white shirt and black tie. 'Food is served,' he bellowed in his deep voice, so loud that the whole of heaven would have heard him. Several jumped in their seats as he startled them, but everyone remained silent still. Then with a loud gong… 'You may eat,' shouted the butler. Again, all were startled by the ringing sound that filled their ears and a little shook up! As he removed the lids off the China bowls, steam rose from the food inside, revealing a banquet that was set out like a feast. Exotic pork loin, with apples, along with crispy potatoes, were served upon each plate, the butler doing a grand job, so Eloise had thought, as soft lighting surrounded the space around her in a cosy glow. A side salad was also available with the meal, and Eloise did not hesitate in accepting some that was being offered to her. Lightly coated with a dressing and with its thinly sliced cucumber was just how she liked it. Dessert was a delicious mango, pear, and ginger crumble, served with fresh cream. Not one person had left even a smidge in their bowl, and as Eloise finished her meal, her gaze drifted towards all the faces that sat around her. It felt so good that she was sitting here with all her loved ones, enjoying great food and excellent company with every relative and friend, not forgetting Will, her beloved.

It was after everyone had finished eating that they spent some quality moments chatting and reminiscing. Eloise stood for a moment on her own and looked around the whole room, grateful for all that she had around her as she smiled to herself.

It had been the greatest family reunion of all.

CHAPTER 22

So much had happened since Eloise's arrival in heaven, from the very first moment she had entered the beautiful, stunning gates, to all the exquisite places she had seen and all the wonderful people she had met. She had learnt so much, too, especially about herself. All the times she had felt so alone, always dwelling on her feelings of loneliness, whereas since being in heaven, she had focused on being with others and helping others, having a connection. She was free from suffering and pain, but instead, filled with joy, and happiness, hope and purpose. She had found solace through trusting others, and all the time they kept reminding her of her worth, it made her worries and anxiety stop. She learnt how to gain comfort and peace, safety, love, and acceptance, because all she had before had been lifted. God was her comfort…

As she closed the curtains in the lounge, she threw herself upon her comfy sofa, covering her body with the tartan blanket that hung loosely over the arm, and as her eyes closed, her mind went into a whirlwind of thoughts, recalling every moment she had spent in heaven and all the beautiful surroundings that embalmed her with warmth, as she reminisced over not only all that she had seen, but all the charming colours and beautiful aromas that had filled her senses. As she nodded off, a variety of visions swirled around in her head. Tranquil images of the lakes and its waterfall, the River of Paradise and River of Life, Pine Forest, the beautiful white sandy beach, Jacoby's Head, Garden of Saint Peter, Fountain Abbey, Eternal Gardens, Golden Bridge, Rainbow Valley, Golden Horizon, and Blossom Garden. The peaceful pictures swiftly moved through her head as more vivid sights filled her mind. Paradise Gardens, the amazing Records Room, the stunning Whispering Sanctuary, not forgetting talking to God at the Temple, and the most important of all, being with all her loved ones.

It was a short while after she had fallen asleep that an unusual sensation ran throughout Eloise's body, a feeling as if she was spiralling, then a sense of being pulled through a tunnel of some sort. There was no noise, just a light, but as fast as it shone with brightness, it slowly faded, as all around her became dimmer and dimmer. She desperately tried to hold on, but somehow, something continued to pull her back the other way, and no matter how hard she tried to keep a tight grip, she did not have the strength, as some force pulled her harder and faster, which told her that something was terribly wrong. Suddenly, an excruciating pain filled her body as a loud noise beeped, like an alarm going off, then a voice called her name. 'Eloise! Eloise!' Slowly, Eloise's eyes flickered open, then shut again, and then she heard it again. 'Eloise, can you hear me? Do you know where you are?' As her eyes opened, then closed again, she mumbled Will's name. Slipping in and out of consciousness, unaware of what was really going on around her, she could only recall that she had been with him, but where was he now! She could not see him or hear him. 'Eloise!' She heard her name being called again, only louder this time. 'I need you to open your eyes.' She slowly flickered them as they opened and closed once more, then, as she scrunched them tightly, a bright light beamed, forcing them to pry open for good, as she blinked several times, trying in vain to open them fully and focus. Bright yellows and oranges stood out all around her, and the smell of what seemed like disinfectant filled the air. The room was silent apart from the beeping sound (supposedly coming from all the machines). As Eloise's eyes squinted to focus, blurred images stood before her, and it had taken a while before her eyes opened fully, as she breathed heavily, her body not moving, but her eyes only, as they moved from side to side. 'Welcome back to the world of the living,' a voice mumbled. Eloise glanced around, taking in her surroundings, still unsure of where she was, but her body ached as if it had been run over by a steamroller and tubes and wires were everywhere, hooked up to something, but she was not quite sure what! In fact, she had no idea what was going on!

The tubes were eventually removed from her throat, and she attempted a shallow swallow, feeling weak and unaware of what was going on. 'Where am I?' Was all she could keep saying, a light blinding her eyes, as her body lay powerless. Waking up somewhere completely different was disorientating and scary for Eloise, and as her eyes opened once more, she felt a sudden confusion fill her fragile body. The space around her that was once full of colour and brightness was now dull, and the air that was once so pure and fresh was now stagnant. She suspected she was lost, in a dream or something, and it was at that moment that she recognised the photo that was slightly scrunched up within her fingers. It was of Will. But why was she holding a photograph of him! Confused even more, as to where she was and what was going on, but all she knew was that where she was now was not heaven… Tears ran from her eyes as they trickled down her cheeks, followed by another and another until a stream flowed down her subdued face as she felt a sudden sadness.

Eloise had been told over the next few days that she had been in a very bad way in a coma for a period, and it had been touch-and-go. So many questions floated around in her head, for she did not know how she had got to where she had been or how she even returned! Then, at that moment, as she glanced across at the window beside her, there was a moment of peace and calmness as she caught a glimpse of a butterfly, and she somehow recalled that same butterfly had appeared several times before at that very window!

She did not remember much about the next few days, not even the visitors that sat around her bed, but she believed what happened to her happened for real and that she did die, for a while anyway, and that her time in heaven would never fade. She believed that being sent there was a gift, although she did not have the slightest idea as to why she deserved it! But she did believe that God called for her to be sent there so that he could free her from all that she was feeling. He had taught her to carry all that she had learnt, as well as holding on to all the love and peace she had experienced in heaven, and carry it always, and she understood also that she had been filled with a new purpose, how to deal with her self-doubt, her losses, her fears, worries and being alone. To understand her emotions, her true self, and what truly matters. She had learnt how to forgive, even when she had not known how to forgive herself and that from now on, she needed to live her life....

Heaven in Eloise's eyes was not just a place where there was no such thing as time. It was a place of freedom. No more stress or upset or sadness. No troubles, no worries. Just calmness and purity. A place of tranquillity, a place of beauty. A place to explore, meeting all those that had gone before and all those that were to follow. Heaven gave Eloise hope and purpose, comfort and peace, positive coping. It taught her how to heal and restore from all her mental and physical health disorders and feel whole. She came to understand that God sent her back because not only was it not her time, but he wanted her to reflect on the lessons she had learnt, take all the love she had in heaven, and carry it to a new start. She must remember, though, always find the right balance, and the strength to heal will follow. Embrace the future, and focus on her journey.

Although grateful to be back with her mum, sisters, and sons, she was, however, sad to leave those whom she had met in heaven. She would always be truly grateful for the opportunity of meeting them all and will never forget them, for they will forever be with her. Eloise knew that where she had been was where she longed to be again and that one day, she would be.

EPILOGUE

Eloise felt Will as the rain poured outside and knew he was with her. She also knew that God the Father, God the Son (Jesus Christ), and God the Holy Spirit were with her....

She comes to realise that Will had never left her at all, he had just graduated to the next part of his eternal journey in heaven, and that at the end of her life, she would join him there and they would have a whole new beginning....

HEAVENS GATE

The day will come when I will meet my loved ones

where the moon and the stars shine like they have
never shone before.

To the place where I can be by their side together
once more.

An open space, filled with the air that I can once again
breathe

A place of peace and healing, where I will never have
to leave.

An undulating beauty that lies before my eyes

as flowers line my path

and cotton wool clouds fill the skies.

Loved ones may no longer be in my life now

but they will forever be in my heart,

and one day we will be together

never again to be apart.

But until that moment comes

I must simply wait….

Wait for the day that they call me home

where we will meet at 'Heaven's Gate.'

-Louise Bourdon

AUTHORS AFTERWORD

I was inspired to write this book due to my beliefs, and I could only imagine what it would be like to be in Heaven.

A glorious place that I hope I will go to when my time comes, and be with all my loved ones…. for real.

A lot of the characters I used in this book are those of my loved ones who have passed away. My real relatives. For example, Kendrick being my dad, Eli being my stepdad. Duke being my stepdad, Alicia, Albie, Bea, and Hendrix, being my grandparents. Jana, my auntie and Terrick, my uncle, plus a few others.

I wrote this book with a vision in mind of what beautiful Heaven is like in my eyes…and I realised that where I had been was true heaven. My heaven. To those who have lost a loved one, I hope you find this book a deep comfort which will inspire you with peace and desire.

The most valued lesson I have found that I have got from writing this book, is that to always appreciate and cherish every moment and memory you get to make, for they are all you will ever have after a loved one has gone.

Take Care   X

ABOUT THE AUTHOR

 Whilst she was born in Swindon, Wiltshire, she was raised in Woking, Surrey, until she moved to Southampton, Hampshire, in 1994. She is a mum to two sons and a nan to six grandchildren. She has always loved writing, and many moons ago, she was very fortunate to have two poems published. 'To love in life…to love in Heaven,' was published in an Anthology in 1996 and 'Baby Mine,' was published in a book called 'The Hidden Grief' in 1998. Due to her physical health and her mental health disorders being diagnosed and getting a lot worse, her writing was put on the back burner, as they say. If she had not already been through enough in her lifetime, sadly, in 2020, her partner John passed away very suddenly, which absolutely broke her. It was then that she turned back to her writing again and wrote 'A Pocket Full of Love' (I wrote this for you). A collection of touching pieces of poetry, in memory of John. Louise then went on to write her next book, 'Broken.' She began writing it in 2021, although she did not complete it until 2024, as sadly she had a stroke in 2022, which not only affected her left side, but she also lost her sight and her short-term memory. A very traumatic time for her. Her dad then passed away in 2023,

which was an added setback to her now fragile body. She thankfully gained most of her sight back, although she still has barely any peripheral vision, but it has not stopped her from writing, and 'Broken' was finally published in 2024. This is a stunning book on a range of her brave poems and short letters from life, to struggles, to loss. Highlighting the hardships of living with her heartbreak, to grieving, to the flashbacks that have haunted her for over 36 years and still do. To the daily battles of her mental health disorders, to her physical health disorders, to her stroke, to her losses, to the sad and distressing times of her suicide attempts, when things have become almost impossible for her to carry on. Louise writes to express her thoughts and feelings, for it is the only therapy that helps her to keep surviving. Her writing gives her the opportunity to tell of her pain and to let her emotions out.

Louise has several more books in the pipeline, which she hopes to complete. A book that was originally going to be a follow-on book from 'Broken,' but she has decided on writing it for others rather than about herself, as she wants to help everyone out there that needs some positive words for their negative days, and another book being a collection of inspirational poems, of encouragement and support, to inspire and soothe the soul. She is hoping that as you turn the pages of both books, the words will fill your heart with warmth and change your life for the better. Not to forget, but to hopefully move forward. To survive…. To live...

OTHER BOOKS BY LOUISE BOURDON

A Pocketful of Love (I wrote this for you)

A moving book of poems written from her heart in memory of her loved one at the time, who sadly passed away in 2020. One of her greatest and proudest achievements ever. But also, one of the most emotional things to, because it was written in memory of John, capturing all the love, life, heartache, and loss in her lifetime with him, which will always be treasured.

This little book of love is all about her journeys with the man she loved and lost, and hopes they will be a source of comfort to those who have also lost a loved one in their lifetime.

Broken

A stunning book on a range of her brave poems and short letters from life, to struggles, to loss. Highlighting the hardships of living with her heartbreak, to grieving, to the flashbacks that have haunted her for over 36 years and still do. To the daily battles of her mental health disorders, to her physical health disorders, to her stroke, to her losses, to the sad and distressing times of her suicide attempts, when things have become almost impossible for her to carry on and with every poem and letter that you read, each will tell a story of how her life has been. Broken is dark and unsettling in places as it conveys the thoughts and feelings of her life. Many things that have never been said. The effects it has on her day-to-day living, making things others may not think about, a bit more difficult.

As Louise shares her life experiences within her writing, she hopes that those who have also felt darkness in their lifetime can read through this and start to realise that they are not alone in their thoughts or challenges.

ACKNOWLEDGEMENTS

There are so many people I would like to thank having being so grateful to everyone's support and encouragement.

To my beautiful, caring Mum... I want to thank you for believing in ME, for believing in this story, for your constant support, encouragement, and love throughout this process. A huge, huge thank you for always being in my life and looking out for me, for always listening, even when I have had moments of breaking down (which is quite often). For always understanding me and trying so hard to keep me positive, and for always being the person I can turn to when my days are dark. None of this would have been possible without you, for you have stood by me during all my struggles, even when you have had your own; you have always had faith in me and have supported my whole writing journey since the beginning. Thank you will never be enough for everything you have done for me mum, and still do for me. I want you to always know that I love you and cherish you more than life itself.

To my lovely stepdad... God rest your soul. You fought to the very end, but sadly, passed away on 2nd August 2025. You were a massive support right from the beginning, and although you struggled as time went on, your smiles and your laughs will always keep me feeling positive. You will always be with me, you will always live on, after all, you are in this book. (Duke).

To my beautiful Aunty... For being the gentlest of souls, you certainly are my mum's sister, and you so deserve to have a copy of this book, because I know we have the same beliefs. I hope that when you read it, it will touch your heart as much as it has mine by writing it. May you glow, as you inhale every single word, and may it lighten your soul as much as it has lightened mine.

To my wonderful Dad... God rest your soul. Sadly, passed away on 19th January 2023. A huge thank you to you for being my dad. For being in my life and giving me so many wonderful memories that I will never forget. You will always be with me, you will always live on, Dad, after all, you are in this book. (Kendrick)

To my amazing stepmum... who is always at the end of the phone, to listen and to boost me up. You have had your fair share of sadness, yet you still know how to make me smile and laugh even when I am not really feeling it myself. You are the strongest woman I know.

To my beautiful sisters... for being such a huge support, for the endless laughter and smiles along the way. Although writing may not be your thing, you always support me with mine and I am so grateful to have you both in my life.

To my brothers-in-law... for caring. Although you may not understand what I am about a lot of the time lol, but have a pretty good idea! Your sense of humour and kindness are real assets, and having you as brothers-in-law has been a real blessing.

To my amazing sons… You have both been my absolute reason for living, making me so proud to call you my sons. Your support and kindness have kept me going, and your funny jokes have made me laugh at times when all I want to do is cry. You always have my back and always know how to keep my head held high, and I shall always be grateful to you for that. You are the two most amazing men ever, who continue to make me so proud for who you are, and I shall always be grateful for having you as my sons.

My wonderful daughter-in-law… We have sat so many times listening to one another's down moments and always understood each other's thinking. We are more alike than we like to admit!

To my six grandchildren… from the youngest to the eldest, but all so very precious to me. You are all so very different in your own way, but all so very special.

To my long-time amazing friend Mags… You have been my absolute rock through everything I have been through even when you have had tough times yourself. Just want to say, how much I appreciate having you as my bestie. Thank you for always been the friend that has been there for me, when all the others have walked away.

To Peter Davey… Special thanks to you, my amazing fiancé, for your constant encouragement and understanding when I was so doubtful with worry as to how this book would turn out. I would not have achieved this without you, so a huge thank you for continuing to believe in me the whole way through. I would never have finished it without your amazing support. You have provided guidance and feedback throughout all my writing, and you have been the pillar of my success. Without you, I would never have believed that there is hope for my future—our future.

I would also like to thank all the lovely lot from the writing group:

Michael Heppell… Firstly, for running such an amazing group, for so long, even though it is not running any longer, and I miss it sooooo much. I am so glad we are all able to stay in touch. I want to thank you, Michael, for giving me the confidence in my writing and for being able to complete this book. My 3rd published book. I would like to express my deepest appreciation to you, because without you, Michael, and write that book, I would never have become an author, it would not have been possible without the support and encouragement from you, so thank you immensely for helping me into believing in myself, even when I have doubted myself for so long.

To all the amazing friends I have made in the group….

Derek Crysell, Sarah McGeough, Lorraine Buxton, Debbie Buxton, Alexis Scott, Belinda Rose Bond, Gaynor Cherieann, Sue Trusler, RKJ Adams, Sally Sindall, Tanith Knox, Denise Montagolo, Jane Somers, and Coral Smith. Thank you for all your support. There are far too many of you to thank individually, but to you all, for believing in me, and what a pleasure it has been to get to know you all. Your kindness and support have touched me in so many ways that I cannot thank you enough.

My publisher, Divergent Mind Books....

I would like to express my sincere appreciation to you for your tireless effort in bringing my book to life and ensuring its successful publication. Without you, the completion of this book would not have been possible. So, a HUGE thank you.

Finally...

I would like to express my deepest gratitude to all you lovely people out there for your support because, by reading this, you are believing in me. A heartfelt thank you goes out to all of you....

One last thing...

May I kindly ask you all, that once you have read my book, could you please, please, kindly leave a review. It will be very much appreciated.

Thank you

x

"Do not let your hearts be troubled. Trust in God: Trust also in me. In my father's house are many rooms; if it were not so, I would have told you. I am going there to prepare a place for you and if I go and prepare a place for you, I will come back and take you to be with me, that you may also be where I am."

John 14:1.3